Shy Girl

KATIE CROSS

KCW

To the makers of the C-tape.

Contents

Chapter One

DAGNY

Dagny: Jayson brought another date into the coffee
shop tonight.

The text flew out of my fingers the moment I could send it
without looking like a crazy stalker woman. Some magic in my
phone sent it across space and over to my best friend, Serafina.

Her reply came seconds later.

Serafina: WHAT?!

A smile slipped across my face at her immediate—and appro-
priately shocked—response, but I stifled it. A quick glance to the
other side of the Frolicking Moose Coffee Shop confirmed that
Jayson Hernandez still sat at the same table where he always sat.
This week, he spoke to a lovely woman with dark eyes and delicate hands that belonged in a diamond commercial.

Dagny: Third date, three weeks in a row, with a
different woman. Comes every Friday night like
clockwork.

Dots appeared on the screen to indicate her reply. So that I didn't look like too much of a slacker, I reached for a rag to wipe down the counter for the third time and prayed no one came through the drive-through.

This was prime-level girlfriend gossip material, here.

Serafina: Coffee as a first date makes sense.

Dagny: You think he's a serial dater?

Serafina: I could see it. He's always been a bit non-committal in the dating world. Do you think he's a player?

Her question swirled around my mind as I stole another glance at Hernandez. Truly, neither of us knew him all *that* well —despite the fact that I went to high school with him and reverentially adored him from the sidelines of my life for almost ten years. Freshman Dagny had serious feelings for Hernandez, the beloved Senior.

Was he a player? No. He *could* be, with those thick shoulders, razor-sharp instincts, and a confidence that carried him places. His way-too-long eyelashes and quick smile certainly didn't help matters.

But he wasn't a player.

Dagny: Doubt it.

Serafina: I feel like we'd know if he was trying to date, so what is going on and why hasn't he asked you out?

A laugh almost bubbled out of me. I shook my head as I replied.

Dagny: How would you *know* if he was trying to date?! That makes NO sense.

Serafina: Mountain life rarely does, I've found. Maybe the girls he brings are friends?

Dagny: Maybe? They aren't from here.

Serafina: The mountains aren't THAT big. None of them are familiar to you?

Dagny: None.

Serafina: I accept this romantic mystery and commit myself to figuring it out.

There was a sense of warmth and friendliness in all the women he visited with, but they didn't strike me as *friends*. Most of them dressed like they had someplace to go—form-fitting pencil skirts. Collared white shirts. Gleaming black hair. Sparkling earrings. If it was a date, why a coffee shop while wearing such glamor? Hernandez was always casual in a tee and jeans. One time he showed up in his deputy uniform. One time in mud-splattered pants and work boots, like he'd been out on his family farm.

Generally I had a good read on people, but in this situation I felt turned upside down. Nothing was clear except the facts.

Jayson Hernandez showed up every Friday at the same time, purchased the same drink, sat in the same seat, and met a different girl. The ritualistic aspect of the mystery killed me. The girls changed every week, arrived in separate cars, departed with a kiss on the cheek after approximately an hour, and nothing else.

Serafina: Is he in his deputy uniform?

Dagny: Not tonight.

Serafina: That's better. You'll drool over him less. He's suuuuuper hawt in the uniform.

In that, she certainly wasn't wrong, but it was time to change the subject. Watching Jayson on a date with another woman was hard enough. Analyzing only led to the same question we had every time: why not me?

Dagny: Are you still madly in love with Benjamin?

Serafina: SO madly.

Dagny: Your life is a fairytale.

Serafina: So is yours. You're just still in the scrubbing floors phase of your Cinderella story. Will you send me a pic of Hernandez and this girl? I need to size her up.

Dagny: That is SO creepy. No.

Serafina: Fiiiiiine. Next Friday, I'll just drop in and we can text each other the way she rates. You know, like he always rates his food? It will be hysterical.

Dagny: Done!

Serafina: How is school going?

Dagny: Almost done with this semester. On track to graduate in December. It's so—

"Hot boyfriend?"

The unexpected voice startled me out of a reply and I fumbled to avoid dropping my phone. With my luck, the whole screen would shatter. Thankfully, I caught it a second before disaster struck in a not-so-graceful fumble that sent a lock of hair into my eyes. Because, of course.

Why not make it impossible for him to see me as anything but an awkward barista? Like I was still fifteen years old, gawping at him from where I hid in the library.

I looked up into a familiar pair of dark eyes. Jayson Hernandez stood there in a button up white shirt with the front untucked, a pair of jeans that fit him a little too perfectly, and the same work boots I saw most weeks. Such a casual outfit belied his natural intensity. When his angular face wasn't caught in a thoughtful expression, it looked like he half-smiled most of the day. Plus, his shorter hair was slightly curled at the ends, and I wanted to run my fingers through the adorable locks.

He blinked, which brought me back to reality.

I'd die of mortification if he saw an entire text message thread about him on my phone, so I clicked my phone off and shoved it in my back pocket.

"N-no." I forced a smile. "N-n-not exactly."

He grinned and set an empty coffee mug on the counter between us. Of the hundreds of mugs on the wall that customers could choose from to drink their coffee in, he'd chosen the one with the Mexican flag. His date had chosen a water bottle, and she tucked it into her purse before surreptitiously fixing her hair in the window reflection.

So what did they talk about over water and coffee? They'd been here almost an hour. No signs of awkwardness between them. Not even indifference or attraction. Just . . . a friendly, neutral air.

Curiouser.

"Thanks again, Dagny." He held up a thumb. "Five stars. Perfect coffee, as always."

I nodded instead of speaking, less out of shock at his proximity—which sometimes happened when I could smell him—and more out of a trained habit not to speak unless I absolutely had to.

He turned to leave with another quick wave and the girl followed.

Once they faded into the darkening parking lot, I let out a gut-deep breath, bent in half, and pressed my forehead to the cool metal of the counter. The chilly feeling against my skin had an oddly grounding response, like a ripple through my body.

No was the only reply I could come up with?

C'mon, Dagny, I silently chided. *You can do better.*

Actually, I probably couldn't. Squeaking any sound out was a win most days. A thousand other words ran through my mind now that he wasn't melting me with his eyes, but I dismissed them. *No* was innocuous, acknowledging, and friendly. He'd clearly asked the girl here on a date. The last thing I needed to do was step in and try to flirt. That always led to a disaster.

How did people flirt anyway?

Besides, my crush on Hernandez had lasted long enough. Years, in fact. It began in high school, when I existed in the shadows and he lived in the limelight. Hernandez had been a senior my freshman year of high school. He lettered in baseball, had a reputation as a kind but disinterested jock, and held a place high on the Honor roll.

He and a group of three other friends had been known for living life on the edge with stupid stunts, and they chronicled all of it through the legendary C-tape. In fact, the ancient C-tape had once circulated past my eyes, and I'd gaped in shock that it had been real. The only way I'd been able to watch it was with an ancient VCR in the library. I'd walked by the back storage room while Jayson and a few other baseball team players laughed over one of the Merry Idiots skateboarding behind a truck while holding a rope.

The C-tape was the only physical proof of some of their idiotic ideas. Skiing down a church with a steep slope. Jumping off 100-foot cliffs. Skateboarding down steep, paved roads on longboards. They even put a ramp on the roof of the local bank and tried to snowboard off of it and onto a jump at the end.

Meanwhile, I'd been known for . . .

. . . nothing.

Certainly *not* my stutter, nor my mom's reputation for crazy, both things for which I'd worked very hard to avoid repute. Anonymity was just what I'd wanted.

When the bell on the Frolicking Moose tinkled, I tucked those thoughts into the back of my mind, straightened up too fast, and my head whirled for a second. Once the dizzy feeling cleared, my gaze focused on a middle-aged woman as she advanced into the coffee shop. Her trembling hand wrapped around a small, black object that was pointed at me.

A mixture of uncertainty, confusion, and terror filled me like a flood of cold water. Was she carrying . . . was that . . . no. While my thoughts attempted to recover themselves, she'd crossed the room and stood a few steps away from the counter.

I blinked.

Yep.

Definitely a real gun.

A designer purse that gleamed with red sequins and gold trim hung from her other arm. Short heels cracked as they walked across the floor, as shiny and red as her purse. Her hair was tied away from her face in a once-elegant chignon that lost itself to tendrils around her face. My gaze darted up to cold, bloodshot eyes and my whirling thoughts fell utterly silent.

"Let's make this easy," she said breathlessly. "All I want is whatever cash you have in the register and a quiet exchange. Then I'll leave you alone."

For a split second, I thought of saying *no*. What would my boss, Maverick, say? Shouldn't I put up some kind of fight? But the urge passed out of me in a moment. No, I wasn't about to go down for a coffee shop. Instead, I stared at the empty, round barrel that faced my direction and swallowed.

"O-o-okay."

Her nostrils flared. The skin around her knuckles was white when she dropped the sequined purse on the counter with her other arm.

"Put it in there."

I reached for the cash register's *no sale* button and pressed it. The drawer chugged out with a high-pitched *ching* and I wondered if I could buy time. To do what? Fight her? Not happening. I hesitated as I looked at the empty slots in the drawer.

She straightened to peer inside the register, then frowned.

"That's it?" she hissed.

My hands began to shake as I calmly reached for what few bills lay inside. $1 bills, two $10, and three $20 came out. I piled them together.

"Q-q-q-qu-i-i-iet n-n-night," I managed to say. Under duress, my stutter became worse than ever. I didn't have the ability to tell her Maverick cleared the till and took the money to the bank earlier today.

Her upper lip curled in disgust.

"Oh r-r-really?" she muttered in a grating, high-pitched voice meant to mock me. "Well that's not enough!"

Her rising shout brought the rest of her hair tumbling around her shoulders. She lifted the gun a little higher so it felt like it pointed right between my eyes. I gulped, able to see the gaunt lines of her face now. At first glance, she appeared to be a striking woman. Now, the truth was so obvious. Too thin. Cracked lips. As if she tried to hold onto a former, healthy, more vibrant version of herself.

A drug addict, maybe?

"Where's the rest?" she demanded.

"C-c-credit," I said. "M-m-most people p-p-pay with cards."

She scowled, then nodded to the purse with a quick jerk of her head. "Put it in." I obeyed, then she motioned to the drawer again. "The coins too."

I scrambled to get the coins out. They felt slippery, as if coated in butter. The promise of the gun sent my mind into a tailspin as I tried to collect the change. I just wanted her to leave. Didn't want this to be real, or my final end. Getting shot in a coffee shop? How could *that* be my life? No, I wasn't this kind of person. I lived a quiet, gentle life. I would not be part of some drug addict's desperate attempt for money.

Just as I gathered the last of the quarters, the door cracked open behind her. The woman's head whipped around in time to see Jayson re-enter. My heart lurched into my throat during the second that it took him to process the scene. Just as the woman canted her hips to swing the gun around to him, my hand shot out. The edge of my palm smacked her wrist and she let out a little cry.

Then she disappeared beneath a hulking blur of white and brown.

The clatter of a gun falling to the floor and a shout of pain followed. Two seconds of silence passed before I managed to ask, "J-j-jayson?"

"Fine," he called. "Call 9-1-1. Tell them what's happening."

I reached for the phone in my back pocket and, after three attempts to type in my passcode, I finally got it right. My fingers trembled as I dialed 9-1-1, then waited while the phone rang dully. Another voice came on the line.

"9-1-1. What's your emergency?"

For a moment, it felt as if my tongue was glued to the top of my mouth. My lips would no sooner form the words *I need help* than my body could fly. The operator spoke again, her voice pressured.

"Hello?"

Panic and frustration made my mind fuzzy until I forced myself to calm down.

There is no pressure for me to speak.

A third attempt yielded no result, which only compounded my desperation. I knew what I wanted to say, I just couldn't get the words out. Not even a squeak or a sound.

"Hello?"

Finally, like a dam giving way, the words exited my throat. "N-n-need h-h-help," I cried. "F-frolicking M-m-moose. G-gun!"

The operator rushed to respond, but I ignored her to scramble around the counter. Jayson lay on top of the woman, the gun barely out of reach. I hurried over and kicked it out of the way as he struggled to get a flailing arm under his control. Once she was fully subdued, and screaming like a wild thing into the tile, he glanced up at me.

"You good?"

I nodded.

"Help coming?" he asked, his face a mask of concentration as he held her pinned to the floor.

I nodded.

"Good work, Dag."

His praise came seconds after the first siren screamed down the street toward us. Red and blue lights whirled outside, seconds away as they barreled down the Main Street in the quiet mountain town of Pineville.

"Wh-what can I d-do?"

"Nothing." He sent me a quick grin, one that I'd seen on a crappy video years ago when I stole a sneak at the C-tape. "I got this."

Chapter Two

JAYSON

My boss, a heavyset woman named Kate, glowered at the floor of the Frolicking Moose. A little smudge of blood the shape of a ring lingered on the tile. She canted her head to the side as she studied it, then made a raspberry sound with her lips. The woman I'd tackled had gone down hard, but she struggled even harder. In the process, she knocked her bottom lip and split it in half.

"New drug, they're saying," Kate said with a *harrumph* like an old bulldog. She shook her head as she attempted to clear the bloodstain with the toe of her shoe. "Something like a cross between an amphetamine with the addictive properties of an opioid. Inhaled, mostly. Reports are coming in from local cities, too. State authorities think it's isolated to a small cell here. No one else is reporting something similar yet."

That information ran through my mind. *New drug.* That's all we needed. Drugs had been an increasing problem in our quiet mountain town for the last several months. New stuff would only draw more of them here and create more issues. I rubbed my jaw, still a little sore from an errant elbow.

"She was freakishly strong on it," I said.

"They all are."

Her dismissive comment nearly set my teeth on edge, but I shoved that off. The high of adrenalin had subsided in the aftermath. The rush seemed to fade faster with each event. Full night had already fallen outside, and after an early morning with a heavy workout, I felt the extent of my fatigue. Not even the cup of coffee I'd finished almost two hours ago seemed to work anymore.

Maybe I was just getting old.

Kate clapped me on the shoulder. "Solid work, Hernandez. We'll get more information soon and pass it on. Let go of it for tonight and have a good night's sleep. You work too much as it is, and you're scheduled to work on Monday."

She left without a farewell, but Kate never made space for that kind of thing. Her mind had already skipped ahead to her next task as she stepped over to Maverick and Bethany.

I frowned while I studied the quiet room. Something here was missing. Except for Kate, the response team was gone. Investigation over. Maverick here.

Still, I missed something . . .

The quiet whirr of the heater was the only sound over Kate's quiet murmur with Maverick. Outside, blue and red lights whirled silently, a quiet, steady beacon like a heartbeat. As macabre as it sounded, the flashing colors comforted me.

That's when I realized it: Dagny.

I'd completely forgotten about her until just then, despite the fact that she was the only other integral part of this equation. She'd remained calm and cool under pressure, just like one of my best friends, Vikram. Couldn't fluster him if I tried. She even managed to get help here just in time. That woman had been strong enough on whatever she'd inhaled that I almost hadn't been able to keep her from harming herself, me, or Dagny.

I rubbed the heel of my hand into my eyes after another fruitless search for Dagny. She lived above the Frolicking Moose now, and had for a few months. Ever since her friend, Serafina, surrendered the lease to marry Benjamin Mercedy. I should go check on her.

But she probably didn't want me to.

My teeth clacked together with indecision. A hot shower and a hard night's sleep sounded best, but the right thing to do would be to check on her. Dagny and I didn't know each other well, but her former work at the Diner, which she'd quit months ago, meant she knew almost as much as I did about Pineville. Which was likely the only thing we had in common, aside from being almost shot tonight.

Certainly wasn't my first time, but I'd bet it was hers.

After another moment of debate, I stepped outside, circled around the back of the shop, and knocked loudly. The entrance to the loft hid a spiral staircase that led upstairs. Lights glowed overhead, illuminating squares of the pebbled ground. A body moved toward the window, seemed to hesitate, and then disappeared. Just before I rapped again, a light moved inside and Dagny came down the stairs.

When she came face-to-face with me, she blinked. Whoever she'd expected, it clearly hadn't been me. For that, I couldn't blame her. Until this moment, I couldn't recall any time that we'd spoken outside of her taking my order or trivialities over coffee. Acquaintances, I'd call us.

But now I couldn't figure out why I hadn't made more of an effort to be her friend. Or . . . *something*.

"Hey," I said through the glass door. "Just wanted to check on you." Her lips round into an O and she attempted a weak smile that failed seconds later. When I realized she wasn't going to speak, I asked, "You good?"

She nodded.

"You did good, Dag."

"Th-thanks. You s-saved the d-day."

I chortled. Preventing a druggie from harming others wasn't, unfortunately, all that unusual for a day in my job. But I remembered again how freakishly strong the woman had been. She could have killed Dagny if I hadn't shown up. Taken from Dagny's perspective, it probably felt like I'd saved the day. Still, it was weird praise to receive because praise had nothing to do with my career motivations.

"No heroes here," I said, "except you. Thanks for your help."

A glass door separated us, and she didn't seem inclined to open it. For some reason, I was glad for that. Women were never cautious enough at night, even in a small mountain town and with a man they trusted. Or allegedly trusted, anyway.

"Are you really okay?" I pressed.

She seemed perfectly composed. Her eyes were clear, no signs of crying. Her voice even, but not stiffly so. Slashes of color crossed the backs of her hand—paint, was it?—and a little streak lingered across her cheek bone, beneath her left eye. All in all, I'd guess she had a regular day, not that she was just held at gunpoint. Except for the quick, hesitant swallow that followed, I wouldn't have known anything was amiss.

She nodded again.

Had I not noticed before how little she spoke? Or was she actually traumatized and just trying to hide it? For some reason, it mattered tonight. My lack of understanding only frustrated me. Dagny was young, beautiful, and clearly had her life together.

Why hadn't I asked her out yet?

"Okay." I nodded and took a step back. She needed space. I could give that. "Let me know if you need anything, okay? I'll bring my card by tomorrow so you have my cell phone, just in case."

Another nod.

"Bye, Dagny."

With that, she disappeared back up the stairs.

Chapter Three

DAGNY

The moment I returned to the loft from Jayson's check-in, I shut the door, slid down the length of it, and collapsed into a heap.

Long, slow breaths calmed my racing heart as I stared at the grains of wood in the floor. The only reason I'd answered the knock was because I thought Maverick and Bethany would want to talk about what happened. Would they be upset with me? Proud of me? Critique my response? There were cameras that they'd already reviewed. Maybe they'd be upset that I gave up the money too quickly.

No, that would be insane.

Maverick and Bethany would be worried about me first. Logically, I knew that, but it didn't prevent my fear. In the end, I just wanted them to respect me as much as I respected them, and I didn't understand why. Even though I dreaded the potential conversation with my employers—and sort of my friends—I still went down the stairs because it was the right, adult thing to do.

Jayson had stunned me right into my usual tongue-tied state.

That I'd managed to get any words out felt like a miracle. Still, he'd left with something of a furrowed brow and an unsatisfied air. As if he'd expected a weeping woman, perhaps? That would be nice. Crying helped *something* come out.

After deep breathing my way through the tightness in my chest, I straightened. The acrid, unmistakable smell of stain filled the loft, despite an open window over the sink that spilled cooling summer air. Broken pallets lay in wreckage across the floor, like discarded driftwood. Metallic containers of turpentine dotted the counter near the sink next to a pile of nails and assorted hammers. A fresh round of stained wood lay propped against the wall. Still tacky, it would be ready for final creation in two days.

I shoved the supplies I'd prepared out of the way and almost knocked a textbook over in the process. The last thing I wanted to do tonight was focus on anything creative or intellectual. Instead, I dropped onto my old recliner. A quiet, vague movie soundtrack filled the loft, so calm I'd forgotten I put it on, because nothing soothed quite like orchestral music. Seconds after I settled, my phone dinged with a text message.

Bethany.

My stomach became a pool of dread, but dissipated the moment I opened the text.

Bethany: I'm so glad you're okay, Dagny. You did everything right by handing the money over. Always protect
yourself first. Money comes and goes, so never worry
about that. Do you want some time off? Ellie isn't
leaving for college for three more weeks. She can cover
you. Or I can, too.

Relief swept through me. Of course they weren't upset. Of course Bethany said the exact right thing. She'd even texted, which I preferred over talking on the phone. Stuttering in person was one thing—the other person could see my attempts to speak and most people were patient. The phone was worse.

Long silences were often misinterpreted, and I ended up talking over people without meaning too, or they did it to me.

Dagny: No, thank you. I'd rather work. Thankfully nothing terrible happened, and I appreciate your words. I wanted to do the right thing.

For a moment, I hesitated over sending it. The last line made me feel a bit like a lost puppy. But then, wasn't I something of a lost soul tonight? Before I could lose my courage, I hit *send*.

Bethany: We are lucky and grateful to have you. Anything we can do, let us know. Mav and I are discussing a panic button that goes right to the sheriff's office. We'll keep you updated.

Dagny: Thank you.

With that weight off my chest, I pulled a blanket over me, snuggled farther into the too-large chair, and sank into a blessed oblivion where Jayson rescued me over and over again.

JAYSON

Almost a week later, my phone buzzed in my hand before I answered a new call. My best friend Vikram's voice brought a grin to my face when he asked, "Hey man, what's up?"

"Hey brother," I said. "Just taking Odin out for a few minutes. How about you?"

A sparkling reservoir lay in front of me as I pulled my cruiser door closed. My Belgian Malinois, Odin, settled in the back after a quick romp in the dry part of the lake bed. We had a full shift ahead of us, and I couldn't wait for something to distract me. Replays of the Frolicking Moose kept moving through my head, and they always ended on Dagny.

I couldn't figure out why.

Why did Dagny fill my head? Why couldn't I stop thinking about her and her level-headed response yesterday? She'd knocked the gun out of the attacker's hand, which might have saved my life. Dagny had always been around, but whenever I tried to peg a specific memory of her, she only appeared in the background.

"Calling about the wedding," Vikram said. "Can you believe this garbage? Grady is choosing to settle into happily-never-having-fun-again at just twenty-nine years old. I mean . . . she's a pharmacist. Her father is a freaking oil tycoon and the wealthiest man in Texas. They're never going to do anything fun ever again."

A pit formed in my stomach. Ah, yes. Grady's wedding. The looming problem on my horizon that I couldn't, apparently, ignore anymore. Considering that the epic island wedding was only a week away, I *definitely* couldn't ignore it.

Grady was the first man out of our four friends from high school—affectionately called the Band of Merry Idiots by our baseball coach—who was just about to succumb to the big ol' M word.

Marriage.

Grady was the oldest of our group by about three months and usually the voice of reason, if *any* reason entered our stupid situations. He lived in Texas now with his almost-wife and we hadn't seen him since our last get together in the winter. He'd been moonstruck and distracted the whole time, refusing to attempt taking a snowmobile off a jump Vik and I had painstakingly constructed over months of work and testing.

"Too dangerous," he said.

And we teased him mercilessly for the next four days.

"Marriage, Jay," Vikram muttered and brought me back to the present before I could respond. "Grady is breaking the pact."

I rolled my eyes. "He is not."

"Might as well be. After this, we can never go back to the way things used to be. He's going to stop coming with us, you know?"

I shook my head in a silent display of frustration. Grady's attention on crazy outdoor stunts had been dwindling for a while as his career gobbled up his life. Helene, his fiancée, was just a matter of inevitability on Grady's normal-life trajectory. That had always been Grady, though. He found a path and never deviated. Not even when his fellow Merry Idiots tried to talk him out of it by scheduling a skydive in Maui.

"He hasn't really been coming for a while, Vik. His heart isn't in it, and you know it."

"But he came enough that it clearly still meant . . . *something*. Helene is going to hold him back. She's going to make him live small and safe in their white-picket-fence world."

"He's making that choice."

"She's encouraging it!"

"Vik, that's not your business."

"He's my best friend. Blood brothers. It *is* my business."

My fingers curled around a familiar scar on my palm. Cheesy, elementary school kids set loose with a dull knife led to all of us slashing our palms and clasping them together in an oath of friendship. As Hollywood as it sounded, something had certainly bonded us that night, because we'd always been together afterward. All four of us crashed through mountain life. Our idiotic stunts are what pushed me into law enforcement in the first place, because I certainly had enough run-ins with deputies. Most of them said to me what I told teenagers now.

"Don't be stupid. Your life isn't worth it."

Only now, I understood what they meant. At the time, I ignored their warnings. Despite my level-headed approach compared to Vikram, part of me felt his same frustration.

Change got us all.

"It's just . . . it sucks." Vik made a raspberry sound, and I could picture him running a hand through his dark, wild hair. "Bastian hasn't said a word about it."

"He's on a fire."

"I talked to him before he went out."

"He liked Helene."

Vik snorted. "He never said that."

"He never *says* that he likes anyone. It's implied if he's giving support. Don't be a hater, Vik," I leaned back in the seat. Sun hammered the roof of the cruiser, warming my face while I turned on the air conditioning. "We always knew Grady would go first. Besides, Helene is lovely."

Vikram grunted under his breath, and I thought I heard a flippant *whatever*. "You're going, right?" he asked.

"I'm going."

"Even with Victoria there?"

Something clutched in my chest, and it felt a lot like stress. Regret. Determination. Idiocy. Victoria was a whole jumble of the lot of them. Grady was my first best friend. He'd bailed me out of so many bad situations, I'd lost track. Grady, to whom I couldn't say *no* and face again without guilt. Grady was as close to a brother as I'd ever get. My single mother had never married after my father died in a car accident at twenty-two-years-old, a month before my birth. My cousins had been my siblings. So had my friends. My sworn-in-blood brothers. It's why I said *yes* when he asked me to be his best man.

Yet Victoria, the annihilistic man-eater of a woman that I'd once chased hard, would be at his wedding.

As the Maid of Honor.

Rock, meet hard place.

Grady's wedding put me in an impossible situation, one that I had only a marginal, small hope of sailing through. Not only did I need to be there to support Grady, but I had to act like nothing existed, past or present, for me and Victoria.

In a word—it was going to suck.

"Even with Victoria there," I muttered.

He laughed darkly. "I hear she's bringing someone new."

"Everyone is new with Victoria." I picked at a string on my leg. "She rotates through men like a swinging door."

"Sorry, Jayce. She wasn't good for you."

My eyes clenched shut. Logically, I knew that. Knew that Victoria was bad news almost the moment I approached her. Could feel it all the way in my veins. But that didn't stop me from being affected. Victoria had closed the door on something happening between us four months ago, yet my pride still stung.

Maybe *that* was why I hadn't noticed Dagny.

I shook my head. No. I didn't need to let my thoughts wander back there constantly. Dagny was . . . something different. She didn't belong in a conversation with Victoria. Dagny had class and grace Victoria would never achieve.

Except, Victoria's presence meant I wouldn't arrive single to that wedding. Not if my life depended on it. Worst-case scenario, I'd take one of my cousins and pay her to hold my hand like we were together, or something. But even that was a path fraught with peril and, as I thought about it, kind of weird.

"You aren't going to bring Maria, are you?" I asked, just to get the topic off of me.

He laughed. "No way. You know she's gone forever."

Vik's ex-girlfriend Maria sent a shudder through me. Her drama-mama attitude had her lashing out like a hissing cat when Bastian met her at a BBQ. He'd responded in kind, and the result had been ugly. The memory replayed through my mind with a cold chill. It hadn't gone well. We'd set Vikram down for a firm talking-to after we'd met Maria and her money-grubbing ways. Thankfully, he let her go immediately. Vik wasn't the "settling" type anyway.

Same thing happened with me and Victoria. Bastian, like a hound, sniffed out our insincere types and sent them running. Like he had a special pulse on people, or something. An unlikely talent for a wildland firefighter who hid away on his beloved computer doing who-knew-what whenever there wasn't a fire crackling around.

Except I couldn't, apparently, avoid Victoria forever. Which had been my original plan when she turned me down. We had no reason to see each other again. Now, Grady's marriage threw a wrench in even that idea.

"Who are you taking?" Vikram asked and broke apart my

thoughts. My initial response of *no one, of course,* almost failed. Last time we'd all gotten together, they'd tortured me with their teasing about my single state. It hadn't been worth enduring twice, which is why I didn't want to go through that again either.

"Oh, you know . . ." I finally managed, "a girl."

The words nearly choked me. If anyone could sense the lie, it'd be Vik.

"You got one?" he asked, his voice lifting at the end. "Hadn't heard you mention anything."

"It's new. You'll like her."

"About damn time, Hernandez. I'm excited to meet her."

I snorted, but decided to steer the subject to safer grounds. "You promoting to Yardmaster soon?" I asked.

"Nah. I like driving the trains too much. Listen, I found a new cliff diving spot while out on the boat the other day. Caught like ten fish, too. You interested? Wanted to try it out but it's never as fun alone."

Flashes of a young teenager that had gone cliff jumping and broken his neck last week surfaced to my mind. I'd been called to the scene to help pull the body out of the lake while his mother, a single woman, sobbed on the shore.

How I didn't die as a teenager, I'd never know.

"Busy weekend," I lied. "Let's try again later?"

"Sure."

His unenthusiastic reply made me wonder if even *he* didn't really care about it, but wanted to save face. In light of his lecture about Grady living *small and safe,* I wasn't sure what to say here.

Were the thrills of our youth dying due to common sense now?

The radio on my dash crackled. My shift was going to start in ten minutes, but I needed a chance to scrabble my brain back together. "Listen, I gotta go, but I'll send you the details of our flight later, all right?"

"Talk then."

The phone clicked off as I closed my eyes, leaned my head back, and sank into the quagmire of problems that had become my social life. Grady's marriage was more than just one of us finally tying the knot, it was the official descent into structure and routine. It was . . . aging out of what we were before. Leaving behind thrills and challenges and excitement.

White picket fences and diapers.

On one level, I totally understood Vikram's frustration with Grady. Grady was giving up the freedom and flexibility of the life all four of us had always loved, but he'd get something more stable and less lonely in return. Rarely did I ever think about marriage or commitment, but Grady had pulled me toward it again.

Now, I couldn't help but at least wonder what I missed.

With a shake of my head, I glanced at my watch. Five minutes to go. Nothing like work to distract me from the looming monster on my mind: finding a date for Grady's wedding.

And she couldn't be just any girl, because whoever I took would be subjected to all three of my idiot friends at the same time. There would be questioning and judgment and vetting, because the boys always looked out for me. Not to mention the potential of drama from Victoria, and all of this wrapped up in a ritzy, Caribbean island package. Whoever I took, I had to be with for days on end.

No, this girl had to be special, and I had three days to find her before I had to finalize the flight, which left in a week.

Plenty of time.

With four minutes left in my shift, I opened my phone and pulled up my text messages.

. . .

Jayson: Hey Char. Coffee again this Friday?

Her reply came seconds later.

Charlotte: Same place as a few weeks ago?
    Jayson: Same time.
    Charlotte: Yep. Xio told me you took her last week. See you there!

Relieved, I tossed the phone into my cup holder, pulled the SUV into drive, and peeled out of the lake bed with my thoughts churning.

* * *

The Frolicking Moose smelled like vanilla and coffee beans when I stepped inside on Friday evening.

Dagny glanced up from behind the counter, her jade green eyes unsurprised to see me there. She didn't bat an eye at my weekly meetings, but did seem curious from time to time. She gave me a quick smile, then turned back to her task. Three pens stuck out of the back of her hair when she spun around. They seemed to hold her brown hair into a loose knot. My brain knotted into a tumble of questions.

Was she still doing okay after the gun incident?

Any sort of PTSD?

Rarely did I know about what happened to people *after* an incident, and even more rarely did I follow up to figure it out. Chasing the adrenaline of those moments was one thing for a guy like me, but how did a woman like Dagny bounce back? She had to work every day in the same place she'd been assaulted.

Maybe that sucked.

Before I could ask, someone approached from my right. A petite woman with dark hair, bright red heels, and sparkling hazel eyes came to my side. Charlotte. She flashed me a quick smile, but turned to Dagny.

"Soy caramel macchiato," Charlotte said.

Dagny zipped to the register, punched in Charlotte's order, and turned to me with a hesitant smile. "A-already g-got yours. B-b-both are on the h-house."

I opened my mouth to protest, my hand halfway to my wallet, but she held up her hand. "P-p-please."

Her eyes had a note of pleading in them, as if there was more to say but she didn't want to say it. I held my breath and silently debated for a moment before I finally gave in.

"Thank you," I said.

Since we'd done this several times before, Dagny grabbed my favorite mug and headed for the coffee. Charlotte studied Dagny closely, then looked back to me, as if startled by something. Then she pointed to her purse on our usual table and started me there with a not-so-gentle shove.

While we settled in across from each other, I tried to pull my thoughts away from Dagny. It wasn't easy. Pitted against Charlotte's flashy attire and sparkling presence, Dagny was more like a down-home friend. She wore jeans, sneakers, and a t-shirt that said *I got your hot beans* across the front.

Charlotte folded her arms across her chest and lifted her dark eyebrows. "*Abuela* says you haven't seen her in three months."

A forced breath came out of me. "I know. I'm busy."

She ticked up a familiar, judgmental eyebrow. "Too busy for your family?"

"No."

Her glare deepened. "If you haven't *seen* her, then clearly—"

"Are you here as her servant?"

She threw her hands in the air. "We all are! It's in the family contract."

I held up two hands. "Okay. Okay. Too busy, no. I just . . . I haven't been around much anywhere but work and . . ."

The words *I don't want to see her* died on my lips.

"She cares about you."

"She chased me with a rolling pin!"

Her lips pressed together in a poor attempt not to laugh, but it bubbled out of her anyway. Then she sobered when I glared. Her ice queen eyes softened. "Sorry. That was a bit strong. I just . . . we miss you. It feels like you're avoiding us."

I am.

Truth laced her words, which made me feel worse, because I certainly wasn't being forthcoming. Yes, I had coffee with one of my cousins most Fridays in a casual bid to avoid the massive Sunday dinner my family had every week. My plan seemed sound. Disappearing off the radar from the family would really incur *abuela*'s wrath, so I didn't entirely leave. With my occasional check-ins, *abuela* could get second-hand information and, for a few weeks, I could act like I wasn't running away.

Clearly, it wasn't working.

The breaking apart of whatever Victoria and I had sent me into a tailspin months ago. At the same time, *abuela* went on a mission to get me married. After setting me up with three dates that utterly failed, she'd chased me out of her house with a rolling pin. I ran like a dog with his tail between his legs and avoided returning as much as possible.

Oblivious to our conversation, as heated as it must seem, Dagny shuffled around behind the counter and drew my attention again. Even though she did nothing, I couldn't help but look at her. Like a dog to a bone, however, Charlotte returned to her original topic. Of all my cousins, she had always been the most persistent. The fault here was mine. Should have asked Xiomara back.

"So, why haven't you come?" she asked.

My shoulders slumped as I sighed. "My best friend is getting married and he asked me to be the best man. Plus I've been doing sixty hour weeks with the drug issues that have been surfacing. And I didn't want to get another lecture on settling down to marriage and babies."

"Which friend?"

"Grady."

She frowned. "Dang. I liked him the most, and you always seemed closest to him. But what does he have to do with the family?"

I sighed. "If I show up to *abuela's* birthday party without a girlfriend or even a *hope* of a girlfriend, she's going to attack again."

Char didn't disagree. Our *abuela* was a loving woman most of the time. She muttered curse words at us in Spanish, threatened us with a wooden spoon if we didn't behave, and sent us home with bellies stuffed full of rice, tortillas, and beans. The only time she didn't forgive our stupidity was on her birthday.

Practically a religious day, she gathered all of her children, grandchildren, and great-grandchildren like a mother hen. All forty of us cluttered their tiny little farm and celebrated *abuela's* life for a full day. That day came two weeks after Grady's wedding, and it loomed like an ugly thing in the back of my mind.

To add insult to injury, *abuela's* health wasn't good. Likely, this would be her last birthday before old age took her. I couldn't believe the old lady had lasted this long.

"Tell me about you," I said and leaned back. Time to get the spotlight off of me and change the subject. Char loved nothing more than talking about herself. "What happened with that internship? You dating anyone?"

I nodded and acted engrossed as Charlotte prattled about an internship in the management department of a craft store and a guy that annoyed her, but couldn't peel my gaze off Dagny and her rumpled perfection tonight.

Why couldn't I take my brain off of her?

Dagny approached and set our drinks down, then followed with a fruit tart and my favorite croissant which I hadn't ordered.

"On the h-h-house," she said.

"Thanks, Dag."

She headed back to the counter before I could meet her gaze, a rogue wisp of hair floating around her temple. I wanted to tuck it behind her ear and out of the way of her eyes.

Charlotte watched her go, then made a little tutting noise under her breath. "She's got the hots for you, *primo.*"

I scoffed. Nah, women were too afraid of me. The whole cop-vibe carried even into life without my uniform. Like we had an aura we couldn't shed, or something. Charlotte made a face that suggested *you're wrong* but said no more. Her gaze followed Dagny behind the counter.

"That's too bad," she murmured as she reached for her drink. "A stutter. Must be hard to work at a place like this when you can't get words out. No wonder she's so quiet. I would be too."

Dagny's shoulders stiffened under my cousins not-so-subtle words. When I glanced over, Dagny's lips had pinched together, but her face was a glass mask, as serene as any I'd ever seen. A rush of embarrassment, then annoyance, flooded me.

"I never noticed," I replied coolly.

Charlotte's eyes widened at my tone, then closed on a grimace. "Oh," she whispered as heat flooded her cheeks. "I didn't mean it like *that.*"

"And yet," I muttered with a glare, "you said it, *idiota.*"

Charlotte cast a concerned glance to Dagny, then mumbled something I couldn't understand in Spanish. Dagny's shoulders relaxed a little, then turned to the drive thru window as a car pulled up.

After Charlotte and I swapped family gossip, ate our desserts, and caught up on her love life—which was far more plentiful than mine—she stood up.

"It's good to see you," she murmured with a half smile. "Please, come back home? We all want to see you."

I nodded.

After a quick hug, she marched up to the counter with all the presence of a bull. Dagny eyed her warily.

"I'm sorry," Charlotte said. "I made a comment about your stutter that wasn't meant to be mean, but probably sounded like it. You present yourself beautifully and I'm sorry if what I said came across as anything else. You're braver than me."

Disbelief colored Dagny's expression. "I-it's f-f-fine," she said, then added a heartfelt, "Th-thank you."

Charlotte smiled, turned with one last nod to me, and disappeared out the door. When I approached the counter with our crumb-littered plates and my empty coffee mug, Dagny glanced at me through her eyelashes. She shoved her phone in her back pocket and straightened up a bit *too* straight. Ah, a guilty face. I knew that better than anything. So what, exactly, had she been texting about?

"Five stars, as always." I pushed the cup back toward her. "Thanks, Dagny."

A smile tugged at the edges of her lips. "F-five s-s-stars," she countered with a glance to the door where Charlotte left. "S-s-tutter comment n-notwithstanding."

I tilted my head in silent question.

"L-l-last week, your date was three s-s-stars. The w-week before that was four, and the w-week before that was two."

Understanding dawned moments later—Dagny was *rating* my coffee dates. I laughed, taken off guard by the witty amusement in her eyes. Then I laughed harder when I realized she'd been rating my cousins . . . and she didn't even know it.

"Fair," I said, thinking back. "Very fair."

Most of my cousins were female. There was only one other male, Miguel, amidst all twenty-something of us. But Miguel and I met over dirt bikes, not coffee. Most of them lived up the canyon, in the bigger mountain town of Jackson City, so she wouldn't know them on sight. Because of that, Dagny probably thought these women were love interests. I doubled over now, laughing harder.

Her nose wrinkled. "H-have I m-missed something?"

"My cousins," I said and wiped the tears out of my eyes. "Those girls are all my cousins, not my dates."

Dagny blinked in surprise, then giggled. Several moments passed before I'd calmed, then I studied her. "How are you?" I asked. "After the crazy lady, I mean. I heard you're pressing charges. Good for you."

"F-fine." She shrugged. "Y-you saved the day. S-sorry I w-wasn't very talkative the other day. I ap-p-preciated you coming to check on me. I was just . . . j-just s-surprised, I guess. I don't always have the words." A tilted smile came to her lips. "I-in a lot of ways."

Her easy nonchalance struck something inside me, and I realized then why I couldn't stop thinking about her.

She reminded me of Bastian.

Quiet. Unassuming. Non-reactive. Sebastian, our thinker, where still waters ran deep. Dagny had that same vibe. The churning in my brain increased, because at one point she'd also reminded me of Vik with her unflustered courage. Something was coming together.

Something that felt a lot like a plan.

"No problem," I said to buy some time. "I'm glad you're okay. You stayed really calm through the whole thing."

"W-without you, it w-would have b-been a disaster."

"I heard a rumor that you're graduating college soon. What's your degree?"

If I surprised her, she didn't show it. "Construction management."

"You want to build stuff?"

She shrugged. "I l-like using m-my hands and b-b-being outside. The m-management p-p-part appeals to me."

"That's fantastic."

She smiled and the final piece came together with an audible *click* in my head. Grady. Her ease of talking about herself and her goals and her love of working with her hands reminded me of Grady. Little pieces of this woman that could relate to every single one of my friends.

My very protective, difficult-to-talk-to friends.

Friends that were intimidating by reputation alone, not to mention stoic attitudes and wild disregard for societal rules— namely Bastian and Vik.

A car pulled up to the drive thru, so Dagny took a step back. "Have a g-good night, J-jayson." She hesitated, as if she were about to say something else, then turned to the drive thru.

Meanwhile, a crazy idea grew in the back of my mind.

And I knew *exactly* what I was going to do.

Chapter Five

DAGNY

The next day, I stared at my mother's dilapidated house. Fading paint. Old porch. The windows were clear of dust except for the corners, but revealed only piles and piles of stuff inside. Tension vibrated through me as I closed my eyes and prepared myself to enter. *This is fine,* I told myself. *I don't have to speak. There is no pressure to have the words.*

I loved my mother and her wild ideas. There was a quality of sincerity within her that few other people had achieved. She lived her life the way she wanted to, and other people could go shoot themselves in the foot—her words, not mine. But trying to get a word in edgewise had always stymied me.

Mom loved to talk.

Unbidden, Jayson's rolling laughter from last night slipped through my mind again. He'd been entirely too attractive while standing in the coffee shop, laughing about something I hadn't clued into yet. The humiliation of my assumption about his "dates" followed shortly after he left and I'd stewed in the horror of it for a bit.

Those girls had all been *cousins,* not dates, and I could have seriously offended him when I rated one as two stars. Mortifica-

33

tion tripled back through me, and I groaned. Now I felt less prepared to face Mom than ever before.

I tilted my head back and took a deep breath. Perhaps I could gather my courage if I just sat here for a few minutes. To marshall my bravery, I slipped to the place I always went when I needed to ground myself.

Airfare: $500
Hotel: $500 for a 3-night stay.
Food: $100
Rental car: $300
Gas: $100
Extras: $200

Location: Fort Worth, Texas.
Plan: Find a social event with Anthony Dunkin and approach him there.

Operation Find My Biological Father had been underway for the last two years. Online college expenses and low wages in the Diner meant saving the requisite $2000 to make this happen took a long time. Things had been better since I moved into the Frolicking Moose. Bethany and Maverick lowered my rent and took it out of my paycheck. The remnants were just enough to pay myself.

That left a small, but heartfelt, savings. I just ignored the inevitable debt of student loans I'd have to chip away at soon.

Money wasn't the hardest part. Tracking Anthony Dunkin down *was*. His location was easy enough to pinpoint because his office wasn't hidden, but finding a place to pop up and say, "Hi, I'm the daughter that came as the result of what I think was a one-night stand, but my mom doesn't talk about it, so I don't know for sure. The daughter you have been purposefully avoiding. Just wanted to say hi!"

Then watch his reaction.

Aside from Jayson Hernandez, I'd daydreamed of nothing else more than the moment I met Anthony Dunkin and he realized exactly who I was.

My eyes flew open when a pair of knuckles rapped on my window. A wild halo of white-blonde hair peered into the driver's side window through slitted eyes that were the exact same shade as mine.

"Why are you sitting out here?" she asked.

A little smudge of fog appeared on the window when she spoke, she stood so close to it. I let out a sigh and reached for the door handle. A bit creepy, with her pale skin, to find her looming outside.

She stepped back to let me out.

"Hey, M-mom."

The door popped open under my hand and she tilted her head to the side. "Come on in. Gotta check my groats."

I trailed behind her through the yard, where free-range chickens clucked and fought each other for scraps of squash littered on the ground. They scattered as Mom strode by, her thin legs taking her quickly through the tall, wild grass and up the stairs. Old flower boxes lined the old mobile home, empty and dry. She had seventeen empty flower boxes now and had snapped at me when I suggested donating some to the cemetery. From outside, the sound of a grinder filled the house, and increased in volume when she tossed open the door.

Mayhem greeted us.

Mom's double-wide trailer had always been chaotic, but her latest idea made it almost unstable. Various food items littered every available space, whether it was bagged whole grain oats—which she called groats—or cans of cinnamon sticks waiting to be ground. Glass jars and linen sacks filled in all the nooks and crannies that food waiting to be processed didn't. A television played somewhere in the background and the scent of incense lay heavy on the air.

Handmade baskets lined with linen filled the kitchen as she waved me past her couch and into the dining area. Bamboo sporks clustered together in fist sized bundles tied by twine. A tag, made of recycled paper, said *Save the Earth with Erika*.

"Just about done," she called over the loud groan of a grain grinder. "The groats got gummy. Kinda wet. Forgot to roast and dry them out, so they're clogging my grinder. Blasted thing takes forever. You almost can't charge enough for ground oat flour with how long it takes."

A giant grinder took up half her old counter space. I paused near the sink, where grain dust decorated the top of the counter. The grinder was at least as old as me. Clear, empty bags lay on the counter next to it, along with more *Save the Earth with Erika* tags waiting to be applied.

Although I'd struggled all the way through high school with my Mom and her strange ways, I'd long since accepted it now. The fact that she managed to single-mom her way through my childhood, put food on the table, and still love me in her strange way felt like a gift. Her eccentricity was sometimes a bit much to process, but she largely just wanted to live her life and be left alone. We would probably never be close, but now that I had adult friends, we didn't need to be.

"H-how's b-b-business?" I asked.

She flipped the grinder off. "Fine. Still trying to get the lease on the old lot where they had that pizza place, remember? Some developer wanted to make it a spa." She scoffed. "Spa. What a waste. Do you know what lotion bottles do to our environment? Anyway, it's about time Pineville sees a store with holistic support and resources, if you ask me."

I nodded and leaned against one wall, my arms folded across my chest. Despite her *holistic* approach to the world, Mom's house looked like a pack-rat's nest. Clogged with miscellaneous old glass bottles and dust. When I had asked her about county and state laws around processing food, she'd rolled her eyes and said, "My bleach bottle and I take care of any problems anyone needs to worry about, thank you very much." I eyed a tottering pile of old newspapers she hadn't taken to recycling yet and thought I heard a squeak.

Mom pushed a lock of hair out of her pale eyes. At fifty-something, she still had a young face, with wrinkles that added character and an intensity in her eyes that felt familiar. Her eyes appeared owlish behind massive, wire-rimmed glasses without which she was almost blind. Beads jangled from where they hung around her neck, scalloping a bright turquoise tank top that dipped well below her collarbone. Today, she wore a pair of old coveralls and slippers made from leather. Normally, she had wispy skirts in various shades of tie-dye.

She studied me. "And you? Thought I heard there was some trouble at the coffee shop."

"F-fine. I—"

"Of course, no information has been released." She rolled her eyes. "Allegedly, the woman was under the influence of some drug. Mark my words, Dagny. They're going to blame mush-rooms again and it's not the mushroom's fault!"

"I—"

"The woman needs to see a better herbalist if she's turning to mushrooms to relax. Marijuana can do a lot these days, you know."

"Mom—"

"Of course, inhaling marijuana is far more unpleasant. Mushrooms, on the other hand . . ."

My mouth opened again, but I closed it again. Why fight it? I let her words run through the background of my mind and kept a very loose track on whatever tangent she'd launched herself into now. Why waste the precious words? Mom didn't actually need or want me to respond. She just wanted to talk.

Like a child who self soothed through chattering to herself. Less than a minute later, she'd worn the subject out.

"Anyway." Mom popped a hand on her hip and lifted her eyebrows. "Any news from you?"

"Ah . . . n-not really. I may have found a place in J-jackson C-c-city that will take my pallet furniture, but I haven't c-confirmed with them."

She frowned. "Why not?"

"I'm b-b-busy."

Frightened, I thought. Mom would pounce on that in a second if I admitted it, however.

"Better get on it," Mom muttered, but turned to pull something off a cupboard above her when the grinder made a screeching sound. "The universe doesn't just give those opportunities away, you know. Gotta take them when they come."

So many replies surfaced to the tip of my tongue, but I stuffed them back down. The universe and I, as Mom saw it, had things to talk about.

"What are you scared of, anyway?" she asked as she riffled through a cardboard box. "Can't be that scary, talking to some local businesses to sell your furniture. We like to support each other, you know. We're in this together."

She said *we* as if she were a vetted business. As if she'd ever worked cooperatively with anyone in her life. Some of her friends bought food or earth-based goods out of her house when she offered a discount, but Mom had never operated above board. Who was she friends with that ran a company?

"I-it's not," I said in an attempt to sound confident. "I-I-I just th-think—"

"I know." She waved an impatient hand. "I know. You don't want them to reject you or judge you based on your stutter, but you need to get over it already."

My nostrils flared as I sucked in a sharp breath. That wasn't what I was going to say, but Mom was forever speaking ahead of me. It's how it had always been and the reason my stutter was so much worse at her house. Her quick *get over it* sent a frisson of frustration through me.

A familiar tension crept up my body, like a fist holding onto my vocal cords. I could feel it tightening, tightening, tightening. Even the muscles in my face and jaw felt the grip. Once this happened, I rarely got my words back, no matter how desperately I tried.

"What can you t-t-tell me about my b-b-biological f-father?"

My firm tone gave me a surge of pride despite the words falling over themselves. By now, I'd normally retreated to uncertain grunts and one-word answers. Several words in a row and a sentence started without a stutter in front of Mom was almost a new record.

Mom paled. The linen bag she'd been preparing to shovel ground groats into fell onto the counter.

"What?" she breathed.

"M-m-my b-biological f-father. What h-h-happened to him? W-where is he? When d-d-did you last talk to h-him?

Although I already knew the answer to most of these questions, I still felt compelled to ask. Her pasty expression didn't improve. She reached back with one hand and propped it on the counter.

"Why are you asking about him?"

A thousand reasons, I thought. *I've always asked them, but never out loud.*

"D-don't know," I whispered.

Which was, in fact, a lie.

I knew exactly why I was asking, but the truth wouldn't cross my lips that way. For most of my life, the questions about my biological father had surfaced and prevaricated around the edges of my mind like a ghost. Regret that I'd asked followed when I saw the firming up of her expression. She wouldn't reveal anything. Short of being drunk, I'd never get this information out of her.

Why did I ask? Did I want to set her on edge? Punish her? I couldn't tell. I just knew the words came out because they'd been sitting there so long.

The last person I'd tell my grand plan to was Mom. The last person that would ever know my plan was Mom. Eventually, I'd never have to ask her anything about him again. I'd know it myself.

She let out a long breath. "I don't know," she said, and pressed her colorless lips together. They'd hardened, impossibly straight, and without an inch of give. I dropped my gaze, cowed by the fury hiding behind her surprise. Likely, the only reason I wasn't getting an earful of words was because of shock.

Which meant it was time to make a gracious escape.

"G-g-gotta go, Mom. My f-f-riend is bringing some p-p-pallets over tonight."

"Yeah, okay." Her shoulders slumped with relief, although there was annoyance there, too. I didn't stop to analyze why, or for what purpose. At least I'd get out of here without being screamed at again.

"H-have a g-good night. L-love you."

She waved me toward the door, and I went willingly. "Love you, too. Thanks for stopping by. Need to figure out this stupid grinder, anyway. How am I supposed to compete with Healthy Foods Market if I can't even make quality oat flour, for goodness sake? Like pebbles, it is!"

Her half-crazed mumblings followed me to the door and out. Once it shut with a firm thud, I let out my first full breath since I pulled onto the property. By the time I made it to my car, some of the dense clouds from my mind had cleared. The ones with my biological father lingering in them remained. Questions about him required moxie I didn't know I had.

If there was one thing Mom *didn't* talk about, it was Anthony Dunkin.

Oil rigs. The current legislation. Overuse and dependence on plastic. LGBTQ rights. She would willingly cover it all and then some with anyone that asked—or didn't ask. Mom had words on words on words, and she never stuttered over them. Never hesitated.

So why did I want to prod her with the remark about my biological father? I'd never really asked before. Not since I was a little girl.

I started the car, rolled the windows down, and drove back to the Frolicking Moose with the wind whipping through my hair. A sense of relief flooding my veins with every mile that separated us. I'd visited Mom this month and wouldn't need to see her for another four to six weeks. At least I had that.

Sometimes, even that seemed far too soon.

* * *

A firm rap on the door to my loft came later that evening.

I trotted down the spiral stairs with a paintbrush in my hand and my hair pulled away from my face by a bandana. An old pair of coveralls that I'd swiped from my old neighbor, Rick, kept me from getting stains all over my clothes. Mom always swore by coveralls, and I reluctantly agreed. They were genius. Still, I reeked like stain and had sawdust on my hands.

A burly figure that waited on my porch had me skidding to a stop a few steps before the door.

Jayson Hernandez stood there, two pallets in his hands. He wore jeans with the knees worn, his usual work boots, and a white t-shirt that stretched too perfectly over his wide shoulders.

My heart cracked like an iceberg, then slid into the depths of my stomach. Two seconds passed before I comprehended him standing there. *Jayson?* Rick said he'd send the pallets over with . . .

. . . a capable person.

The old man had a meddling hand, because I was certain he had nothing in his schedule to prevent him bringing the pallet wood himself. No, he'd wrangled Jayson into this on purpose, and I'd have words—actual words—with the old guy. While dreaming of my revenge, I cleared my throat. With a muttered curse, I forced a smile and pulled the door open. Jayson responded in kind, looking a little less certain now that I'd gawped at him like a cavewoman.

"Hey." He nodded toward the two pallets. "I have ten more of these that have your name on them. Is that . . . is that right?"

With a nod, I opened the door wider.

"Th-that is c-correct."

Silent questions filled his beautiful, velvet eyes, but he kept them there and yanked a work glove back on his right hand.

"Lead the way," he said.

I peered around his more-than-capable shoulders. Behind him was a clunky old work truck likely from his family farm. Or maybe that's what he drove. I wasn't used to seeing him outside his cruiser. Pallets were strapped down in the back.

"I c-can grab some others—"

"Nah. I'll get them later."

To avoid the problem of finding my brain and forcing it to figure out words yet again, I nodded and gestured him up the stairs. While he stepped ahead of me, despite the awkward navigation of pallets on a spiral staircase, I used all my willpower not to study his jean-clad backside.

The universe sure tested me.

He stopped just inside my loft and set the pallets off to the side. A bit of a mess greeted us upstairs, although I prided myself on my usually clean living space. Cans of stain and turpentine, half-broken crates, splintered wood, nails, and hammers littered the floor of over half the loft. Aside from a bed that Serafina had left behind, I didn't keep much in here. Something about open space made me feel like I could breathe better. Functionality was so much better than . . . stuff.

Or maybe I just didn't want to live like Mom.

"What have you got going on up here?" he asked with a nod to the pile of debris. In the midst of it was a new piece of furniture that I'd attempted to sketch out on an old chalkboard secured to the wall. Various shades of chalk colored the surface, each assigned a different purpose. No one had ever seen my workspace before, except Mom.

"I-I create furniture from p-pallet wood." I waved to the half-spawned creation in the middle of the room that hadn't quite come together the way I wanted it to. "I needed to m-make some extra money in high school to b-b-buy a car, but I didn't have many options. S-s-so I found some old pallets and st-started to . . . make stuff. I still d-do it now for a . . . p-project I have."

Even me saying the words *high school* made my heart flutter. Did he even know we went to school together? The mountain school world wasn't *that* big, but we were grades apart. If he did remember, then what did he recall about me? I shuddered to think.

Jayson advanced into the room and circled my little wreckage of creativity. Heat crawled up my cheeks at the thought of him judging my work, but I kept my chin tilted back. Showing it to Jayson was good practice. If I wanted store owners in Jackson City to sell my woodwork, wouldn't they also inspect and judge?

No, it would be different.

He stood up to better inspect a particularly flaky piece of wood. Somehow, it felt more intimate and scary with Jayson running his finger along the edges. Like he peered into my soul as if it were a crystal ball.

"That is so cool," he said.

"W-what?"

"This is awesome." He grinned and gestured around us. His gaze fell onto the far wall, where Bethany had helped me stage a few of my finished works so I could take photos to send to the businesses that I wanted to sell them. "*They* are awesome."

"It's . . ."

Sort of desperate, I thought. The pallet furniture was a means to make money to meet my biological father. A man that, for all intents and purposes, didn't want me to exist. The fact that I wanted to force him to acknowledge me was desperate enough. Scrapping together furniture out of pallets? Seemed a step farther.

"Inventive," he finished for me, and said it firmly. I didn't have the courage, or ability, to correct him or try to change his mind.

The need for funds hadn't diminished over the years, which is why I continued to play with pallet wood design today, although I was in a far better financial position than I'd ever been before. Maverick and Bethany paid a generous salary for a barista, and I felt certain they cut the rent down on the loft when I applied. Why they'd be so kind to someone they hardly knew and were not obligated to help, I had no idea. Nor did I question it, because being a barista gave me the space to try out the pallet furniture.

"Th-thanks." I stepped farther into the room. "I'm p-p-prepping a few pieces to see if they'll s-sell in Jackson City."

"Sweet."

He said it low and quiet, as though with reverence. His enthusiasm seemed sincere. He ran a hand over one of the projects that I'd recently set aside out of sheer frustration and a need to unblock the design in my head. The plans for a chair with a pull out drawer on the bottom and shelves on the sides seemed so clear in my mind, but hadn't puzzled together the way I wanted it to be in reality.

Which was just *so* like life.

"You're sanding each board?" he asked with a glance to the powder on the floor. Was that surprise or curiosity in his tone? I couldn't tell. I chewed on my bottom lip before nodding, uneasy at his questions. No one had ever cared. Beneath my surprise, however, was a layer of excitement.

Someone *cared* about my pallet work!

"Yes. A p-planer would be so much easier," I said, then let the rest of the sentence drop. *But I can't afford to buy more tools. Not until I know this furniture will sell.*

"Do you have a hard time getting the boards to match evenly?"

"S-sometimes. P-p-pallets are more rough than uneven." My fist flexed at my side, where bandaids dotted different fingers thanks to slivers from a particularly rough batch Rick had sent. "The s-s-s-sanding is . . . k-kind of annoying."

He smirked. "I bet."

Jayson crouched over a few pieces again, his gaze darting around as he inspected the whole mess. His interest surprised me. Did he like to work with his hands? Build? For me, piecing things together with hammer and nails had been more than a hobby growing up. It had been the only way I could create safety and escape. Tree houses. Forts. A bed with room to crawl underneath it. Anything to create structure in a world that felt as loose as jello.

Now, my penchant for fiddling with board and nail and hammer could be the answer to . . . well . . . *me*. It would provide the extra income to get me to Texas and close this gaping door in my life.

Jayson straightened and put his hands on his hips. I swallowed hard and turned away so my gaze didn't idle on the broad shoulders or perfectly sculpted chest beneath his casual t-shirt. Seeing him without his deputy uniform made him so totally . . . normal.

"Do you take custom orders?" he asked.

"S-sure?"

His eyes glimmered with amusement. He shot back, "Is that a question?"

"Yes."

"Have you never received a custom order?"

Heat returned to my neck again. "Ah, yes I have. B-b-but it wasn't in p-person. My friend, Rick, got it f-f-for me."

A calculating gleam appeared in his eyes, one that made it seem as if his thoughts were a thousand miles away from here. When he blinked back to the present moment, the hair on the back of my neck stood up.

"How much family do you have?" he asked. A note of the sheriff's deputy lingered in his tone, as if he were about to interrogate me.

"Why?" I asked and realized I'd taken a step back. Nothing in my life was exciting enough to take note of, nor was any of it hidden. Likely he knew almost everything about me just because he was so involved in the town.

"You're an only child, right?"

Reluctantly, I nodded, even though he'd ignored my question and asked me a second one. Something in the gleam of his eyes had me curious.

"Cousins?"

I shook my head, still bewildered that I had his cousin situation *so* wrong. I'd even gone to school with one of his cousins, although the rest had moved to Jackson City much later, after he'd graduated. They didn't come around here very often.

Obviously.

He nodded, as if affirming something to himself that I couldn't hear. But what could the size of my family possibly have to do with anything in his life? And why did he seem so excited all of a sudden?

"Are you a woman that can appreciate the toss of a dice?" he asked. That conspiratorial gleam that had made so many girls swoon in high school reappeared now, and my stomach clenched. Traitorous body, even *I* was still affected by his roguish grin. There was something boyish in the shape of his face, though his stature had nothing young about it.

"W-what does that mean?"

"Do you ever take a chance?"

Not yet, I thought, and my mind slipped to Anthony Dunkin, and then back again. Jayson stared at me so intensely I couldn't look away. My breath paused while I thought the question over.

Wasn't every day a toss of the dice?

"I will," I finally said.

One side of his lips tilted in an adorable, quirky grin that stole all the rest of my breath. "Will you go on a date with me? And by date, I mean an adventure to my best friend's wedding where we'll be together for three days, sleep in the same hotel room, and pretend to be a couple when we're really not."

Chapter Six

JAYSON

The utter silence that followed my question sent my heart into my throat.

What had I just done?

For what felt like an eternity, Dagny just stared at me. Her lack of words had nothing to do with her speech impediment this time. A layer of shock glazed her eyes and I felt the weight of it all the way to my bones.

Bad idea.

Really bad idea.

My mouth opened to retract it and save my pride. To tell her that was a joke and I wanted to see what she'd say, but before I could muster the strength—or was it desperation?—to say anything, a word slipped out of her mouth on a squeak.

"What?"

Too late now. It had been acknowledged. Besides, I wasn't the kind of guy that backed away. Once I started, I must finish. But where to start? How did I explain such a delicate and over-whelming situation? There were so many people I didn't want to hurt here. With the right finesse, I could come out of this mostly intact.

If she agreed.

"I need some help." The admission felt like a stone in my throat, but I couldn't take it back either. Besides, maybe it needed to be said. The strange angles of what this upcoming weekend had become were tightening like a noose around my neck. I couldn't deny it was true, anyway.

To my shock, she softened. Her brow lowered slightly in a silent question. Taking it as permission, I continued.

"One of my best friends, Grady, is getting married, and he asked me to be the best man. Of course I accepted."

My hair stood up on end as I ran a hand through it. Dagny didn't say a word, but her eyes seemed to be processing it in the background, as if I could see her brain working through everything I said. So I kept going, because that silence needed to be filled.

"But that was before I realized that a woman named Victoria would be there." A pit fell into my stomach just thinking about her. "I . . . sort of dated her. We didn't end well and she's best friends with the bride. Anyway . . . I just . . . I don't want to go to Grady's wedding alone with her there. She's moved on to someone else and I don't want to show up by myself."

"W-was it that bad?"

I snorted. "Yes, but it could have been worse. Besides, going to Grady's wedding without a date?" My eyes rolled in the back of my head. "His mother will set me up with every bridesmaid or every other single woman at the wedding just to save me from Victoria, and that would be even worse."

Her eyes lit up with a smile. "P-p-probably."

Her affirmative response gave me pause. Did she know Grady? Most people in this area knew his family, at least. She must know his mother to agree with my statement so warmly. How old was Dagny anyway?

I brushed that aside for later.

"It would just be a lot easier if I took someone with me," I concluded. "I won't miss this just because of Victoria and because, well, they're my brothers. We take care of each other. And that's the other thing."

Her eyes widened. "Th-there's more?"

"Sort of." I bit my bottom lip, then sighed. This was a disaster, but I was too far into it to go back now. "My friends . . . they can be hard to impress, for lack of a better word."

"Oh?"

Uncomfortable with just how to phrase this, I rubbed a hand over the back of my neck. I had a feeling they'd love Dagny, but how to say that?

"I . . . I think they have my best interests at heart, they can just . . . be sort of . . . intense when they meet girlfriends."

"Int-tense l-like a-a-asking a lot of questions?"

"Yeah." I nodded. "They've asked a lot of questions in the past."

"A-a-are they r-rude?"

"No."

She made a noise in her throat, and a puzzled expression followed. I sighed and played my next card, which, fortunately, was the truth.

"I know you'll pass." I lifted up a hand and let it fall again. "I know they would love you. It's part of my selfish ask. You are the kind of person that would make things so much easier on me. Even though we don't know each other very well yet, I think we could have fun. Even if we just lay out on the beach all the time."

Dagny blinked and let out a long, long breath. When it finished, she paused there in a sort of puzzled state for several moments. I shifted my weight. My mind raced with thoughts but none of them would settle. Had I phrased that right? Or was she going to laugh me off and call me insane? I wouldn't blame her. The sheer amount of thought behind her eyes gave me hope. Because this *was* insane, but it was also sincere. I needed help, as hard as it was to admit. Maybe that would count for something.

"W-why m-m-me?" She gestured helplessly to herself, as if to say, *why would you do this?*

"Because you're so impressive. You're real. I know you'll fit right in."

She scoffed, and I sensed some weight behind that. Before I could ask, she said, "B-but I s-s-stutter."

I shrugged. "So?"

"S-s-so won't that emb-b-barrass you?"

"No."

An expression twisted her face that I couldn't read and didn't even try to. If she wanted to go, she'd do it. If she didn't, she wouldn't. Regardless of what she said, I'd figure it out . . . but it would be a *lot* easier if she were at my side.

"W-why fake it?" she asked next. "Y-you're a catch. W-w-why don't you h-have a g-girlfriend?"

It was my turn to be shocked. The question was fair and one I should have anticipated, but more than likely I just tried to avoid. "Ah . . . because I don't make time for a girlfriend, I guess."

"M-make it?"

"Yeah. I could find time but I haven't." I shrugged again. "Don't know why."

She nodded and licked her lips, seeming lost in thought. Just when I thought I'd lost her, when I was certain she'd smile in her kind, quiet way and thank me for the flattery but it wasn't her thing, she asked one more question.

The one thing I'd saved as the ace card.

"W-w-where is it?"

"Grady happens to be marrying the only daughter of the wealthiest man in Texas. They are having the wedding on an island somewhere in the Caribbean."

Her eyes widened. She paled.

"The w-wealthiest m-man?"

"Dunkin is his last name, I think."

"S-seriously?" She reached over to touch the wall, as if thrown off equilibrium and about to drop. I studied her for a moment. Did she have a thing against rich people? Was it her stutter or something?

"Yeah," I drawled. "I'll pay for the flight, of course. You won't have to pay anything. You'll get a free trip to a beautiful Caribbean island, but you'll be there with me as the only person that you know. Grady and Helene have mostly invited close family. The whole wedding guest list is something like a hundred people."

She'd gone oddly still for several seconds, then slowly sat down, her expression pale. Her lips wordlessly formed a question, but no sound came out. The hair on the back of my neck stood up in alarm. Something wasn't right.

"You okay?" I asked.

She waved me off when I took a step toward her, then stopped. Her lips pressed together until they blanched.

"Dagny?"

"F-f-f-fine," she whispered. "J-j-just . . ."

She trailed away. Her unseeing gaze stared right at her phone, which lay on the ground in front of her, as if it were about to swallow her.

"Are you sure? Can I get you something?"

She shook her head, neck taut. "N-n-no. Thank you. C-c-can I think about it?"

"Of course."

I stepped away to give her space and the scrape of wood against the back of my thigh reminded me why I was there. The pallets. This whole weird night was only supposed to be me dropping a few pallets off at her place, not leaving my messy problems onto her lap to help me solve.

"Let me get the rest of your pallets," I said, and she relaxed.

Space, I realized. She just needed some space. Without looking back, I headed back down the spiral staircase, my thoughts a whir. Just to give her the time she needed, I didn't hurry. When I returned, she stood at her sink near a half empty glass of water. Both thumbs busily typed away on her phone. Although dying to know who she texted, and what the odd reaction was about, I forced myself to turn around and leave, again.

When I brought the last pallet up the stairs, Dagny turned to face me again. Whoever she spoke to had clearly helped, because she had her head tilted up and an expression of determination now. Any shock or hesitancy had been wiped away.

"You good?" I asked, for lack of anything else to say.

Dagny nodded and a small smile made its way through. "Yeah, th-thanks. I-I-I'll go."

"Seriously?"

She nodded again.

Until the relief flooded through me, I hadn't realized just how much I'd been hoping for her to bail me out of a situation that became progressively worse with every passing day. Not only that, but I *knew* the guys would love her.

"I . . . I'm n-n-nervous that your f-friends will . . . w-w-well, it'll be fine." She pulled her bottom lip through her teeth with a sideways shrug, as if to say, *what can I do?* I resisted the urge to put a hand on her shoulder.

"They'll be your new best friends," I said.

To that, she had no reply. Instead, she held up her hands, which were clasped with each pointer finger pressed together and lifted as one.

"I-I have three c-conditions. F-first, I-I have s-something I need to d-do while I'm there a-a-and I don't want to a-answer any questions about it. Y-you have to l-let me go and d-do it."

I frowned. "Will you be safe?"

She nodded.

Although I didn't know why I hesitated, I did. Something in her expression gave me pause. After years working in law enforcement, I'd learned that my gut knew more than I did and I listened to it all the time. Tonight, it told me something was up. But there was no getting to the bottom of it tonight. The ferocity in her expression wouldn't go away soon. As a deal-breaker, it was an easy request to grant.

Still, I didn't like it.

"Okay," I said.

She nodded and let out a long breath. "S-second: you can p-pay for my ticket b-but I won't l-let you p-p-pay for everything else. I-I can pay for things too."

Shock almost rendered me speechless. She had to be kidding. She wanted to grant me the biggest most trusting favor in the world, then pay for herself? Oh, no. That's not how the Hernandez family worked.

"I appreciate that." I shook my head. "But this one is all on me." Before she could argue, I held up a hand. "Dealbreaker. You're giving me a huge gift, so I get to pay your way."

Her nostrils flared, but she finally gave up with a roll of her eyes.

"F-fine."

"The third condition?"

Her gaze slammed right into mine. "N-no lies. I'll g-go as your f-friend, but not as a f-f-fake girlfriend. It's not how I r-r-roll."

A hundred thoughts slammed into me all at once, then knotted into a tangle of emotions I shoved aside. Amongst it, however, was a sense of gentle chastisement I couldn't help but feel to my bones. Without meaning to do it intentionally, Dagny had just put me in my place.

Oh, yes.

The boys were going to love her.

"Deal," I said.

Dagny blinked, as if she'd expected resistance, and then nodded. I stepped back. "I'm buying the tickets as soon as I get home. I'll text you the details. While we're on the plane, we'll lay out the information and decide . . . everything. We leave Thursday. Can you get the time off?"

"Sh-should be fine."

I grabbed the doorknob behind me and said with all the sincerity possible in my body, "Thank you, Dagny. This is . . . it means a lot."

A fleeting expression passed through her gaze before she nodded, a hesitant smile on her face.

Without another word, I turned and headed down the stairs to finish up the pallets.

Chapter Seven

DAGNY

Clouds littered the sky beneath the airplane where I sat, dotting a green earth with white puffs. In disbelief, I swallowed hard, then turned to stare at the back of the seat in front of me. For the first time in my life, I was in the *sky*.

My first airplane ride.

With Jayson Hernandez.

To a tropical island.

This couldn't possibly be real.

Behind me, I left a studio attic full of broken-down pallet wood that was supposed to earn me the money to do something just like this. Ever since I accidentally stumbled onto Mom's non-disclosure agreement with Anthony Dunkin and my whole world flipped upside down.

Now, a wild opportunity had landed in my lap.

There were a thousand things I already feared about a trip like this. Being seen in my swimming suit. Laughed at for my stutter—or even just *tolerated* or *avoided* because of my stutter. Sometimes, utter rejection was easier than people being polite but frustrated with how long it took for me to get words out. Not to mention the looming truth that hung above it all. The ugly monster. The real *reason* I had said yes to Jayson's insane plan. My unknown, absent, biological father would be there.

Because he was the father of the bride.

A copy of the non-disclosure agreement signed by both my mother and Anthony Dunkin lay tucked into my bag, where it would remain until I found the perfect opportunity to approach Anthony and hand it over. I wouldn't say anything to his wife, and I wasn't here to out anybody. I didn't want money.

I just wanted some acknowledgment.

The sheer audacity of showing up at this wedding made me more nervous than anything. I just wanted to see him. See what kind of person he was. See how I felt when I stood before him. See what it was like to face the man that influenced my world so much for how little he was in it.

Although I'd had three days to get used to the idea of traveling to meet my biological father with Jayson, I'd just avoided thinking about it. Avoided Serafina's text messages, her squeals of excitement when she stopped by and I updated her on everything. But I stopped my denial long enough to take her clothing advice. New swimsuits, cover ups, and shorts packed in a bag somewhere in the belly of the plane completed several possible ensembles. Besides, I'd never been to an elaborate wedding like this, and the thought of elegant dresses had been too daunting to tackle alone.

My hands clutched the arm rests as the plane gave a little bounce that jolted me out of my thoughts. Lights popped on over the seats ahead of me, then off again. On the aisle seat, Jayson riffled through a magazine he found stuck into the plane pocket in front of him, then shoved it back in the pocket. His leg bounced restlessly. Apparently, he didn't like being locked into a metal tube tens of thousands of feet above planet earth.

I kept my eyes straight ahead to avoid awkwardly staring at him. My mind still rotated around my main tenet of disbelief in this whole mess.

What was I thinking?

For one, I'd been thinking that I'd have a free ticket to meet my biological father. On the other hand, a small hope that I could humanize Jayson and stop being so obsessed with him arose close after. Would my obvious focus on him wane if we spent too much time together? I certainly hoped so.

My stomach churned yet again. I still couldn't comprehend that such a strange circumstance was real. That Jayson Hernandez asked me to go to a wedding with him, where the father of the bride happened to be my biological father whom I'd been hoping to meet for years.

My thoughts fragmented again, the way they did when I tried to comprehend this disaster. Would accidental sperm donor be a better word? The whole mess made Helene my sister of a sort, and she knew *nothing* about me.

Anthony Dunkin had been a blip in the timeline of my mother's life. Likely, a one-night stand that resulted from a drunken tryst while Mom was on vacation in Texas, although details were sparse. From what I could discern through tracking down dates and internet searches, he was married at the time to the woman who remained his wife. At what would have been two months pregnant, Mom signed a non-disclosure agreement on advice of his attorney, and he gave her a consideration of $50,000 to never say a word about him.

Mom had kept her end of the bargain, but she hadn't hidden the non-disclosure agreement well enough. Which only made this all that much crazier.

What if I looked like Anthony more in person than what photos revealed?

What if he knew me when he saw me?

The latter possibility seemed nearly impossible. The man left my life when Mom was less than three months pregnant with me. How would he ever know me? Although I couldn't deny the very distant, remote possibility he'd recognize something in me. Mom hadn't lived in Pineville at the time of the affair, so he'd never know to connect her to a place. Maybe he'd recognize me in her? Him in me?

The odds of him finding out who I was were almost non-existent. I just wanted to *see* him. Observe him in his life and with his family. See what kind of man brought half of me to the table and then walked away with a $50,000 consideration and never looked back.

More importantly, I wanted him to see *me*.

Maybe the whole mess would all make sense once I met him. He wanted to keep his secrets hidden because his life was so lovely and perfect. Maybe I'd feel a sense of relief—or betrayal—in what would never be. The other haunting questions of my parentage, the really vulnerable ones, would always be unanswered.

Did he think about me?

Did he regret not knowing me?

Was he ashamed of me?

Even days after Jayson revealed Anthony's name, I felt stunned by the cocktail of fate that played out in my life. What were the odds that all of us could be so interconnected? That strange situations and circumstances could bring us full circle this way? It seemed almost too bizarre to be real, but then . . . how could it *not* be real?

As if all that pressure wasn't enough to deal with, I had to throw Jayson Hernandez on top of the pile. My throat tightened as I thought about how this complicated maze would all play out between me and Jayson. Not well for my part, I'd bet. He'd be in a tuxedo or swimsuit at any given moment. With his quick, warm smile and that boyish expression, I'd drown.

At least Jayson had agreed to go as friends. Stuttering was hard enough, but my conscience made it worse. I was unable to speak when I lied, and would have been a horrible mess pretending to be his girlfriend. As lovely as the dream seemed to be, the reality was far less functional outside my head.

Something Serafina said whispered through my mind as the turbulence calmed. *Can't you just enjoy this opportunity? You'll be with Hernandez! There's no one safer or more gentlemanly than him.*

Which had truth in it, or I never would have agreed to come with him.

But *enjoying the opportunity* seemed *so* dangerous, like intentionally flirting with fire. Yes, I could enjoy my time with Jayson as a friend. At least show affection enough to keep Victoria and others off his back. My heart would be a ragged mess on the other side, however, when we both went back to our individual lives and I was just Dagny again.

Wouldn't it be a ragged mess anyway? I would meet my biological father without him knowing it and the only reassurance I had in this entire scenario was that Anthony Dunkin would finally be forced to face me. The mistake he tried to avoid.

In the end, however, Jayson did me a big favor. Bigger than what I did for him, which gave me a twinge of guilt that he felt so obligated to pay me back. Jayson had eliminated all my obstacles to finding Anthony and taken me right to my goal, and he didn't even realize it.

"You doing okay?"

I jerked, brought sharply out of my thoughts by the mild concern in his voice. When I glanced over, Jayson studied me.

"F-fine. Thanks."

He seemed reassured by my smile, but not by much. "Ever flown before?"

I shook my head.

"We'll even out in a minute." He leaned back, at ease in this world. "Did you have any problems getting the time off?"

"B-bethany was happy to give it to me. Sh-she's been worried after the . . . the c-crazy woman."

"Good. I'm glad."

"W-what happens after we a-arrive?"

"We'll have a few hours to get settled in our rooms. I called Grady and asked for separate ones for you and me. Then there's a big welcome dinner on the beach tonight."

He leaned a little closer and the heady, spicy smell of peppermint moved with him. He hadn't shaved the night before, so stubble darkened his jawline. I tightened my fingers together as he pulled his phone out of the pocket in front of him.

"Here's the hotel we'll be staying at on the island," he said. "You gotta see this place. It's unbelievable. They booked out an entire hotel, so no one else will be on that part of the island except the staff and the wedding party. Isn't that wild?"

"C-crazy," I murmured.

He angled the screen of his phone toward me and scrolled through a browser he'd clearly pulled up before we took off. Glittering sapphire beaches, white sand, poky palm trees. They slipped by in a blur of color and light and brightness that I couldn't help but feel a heady excitement for.

"It's am-mazing," I said.

He grinned. "A welcome break from real life, for sure."

My fast joy fell for a moment when I realized just how little I knew about the situation we'd step into together.

"T-tell me about Victoria? W-what happened with her?"

His expression shortly followed suit. Jayson frowned, smudging the delight that sent butterflies all the way through my body. My toes tingled in the aftermath, still. At this rate, I'd never make it through the weekend.

"Victoria," he said, flicking the consonants off his tongue. "It's a weird story. We met when Bastian and I first flew out to meet Helene, before Grady proposed. Vik is a train conductor. He had already visited Grady when he drove a train to Texas on some deliveries. Victoria came with Bastian, me, Grady, and Helene to dinner one night, and we hit it off."

His voice gained the distant quality that storytelling always lent, and I wasn't surprised to see the story play out across his expression to match his words.

"I stayed for a week, and Victoria and I spent all of that time together. She lived with Helene's parents for a while after graduating college with her Masters in business or something." He waved that off with a shrug. "There were no real commitments between us, but we both seemed to feel something. I thought we did, anyway. Turns out that wasn't true."

His candidness startled me. Rarely did I meet someone this open about who they dated or . . . didn't date. Then again, maybe it was *me* that kept things hidden so long.

"Wh-what happened?"

He shook his head. "She basically told me off. Said there had never been anything and never would be. As a deputy, I couldn't support her lifestyle."

My mouth dropped. "You d-didn't m-make enough m-money?"

A wry smile showed on his face. "Exactly."

Several seconds passed while I comprehended that, but I took it for the warning I sensed in his words. We were about to enter the world of wealth, resources, and getting ahead. Even if this trip was just for a wedding and I had no ties to anyone there but Jayson, I already felt overwhelmed.

"Y-yikes."

"Same feeling. She's bringing a new guy with her to the wedding and I just didn't want to be there alone if she had someone else. That's all."

I gave him a little, reassuring smile. "I'm g-glad to b-be here. Sh-should I be worried ab-bout her?"

"Nah." He shook his head. "No one's getting near you, Dag. I got you."

The edge of uncertainty in his voice told me he wasn't entirely sure, which meant I could expect any number of things at this wedding. A little thrill charged up my spine at those words, anyway. *No one's getting near you, Dag. I got you.* Those would replay through my mind for my entire life.

Victoria didn't bother me, which was a relief. She'd probably ignore both of us for the new guy she'd bring along, since she seemed to have so many. I drew in a deep breath and steeled myself for the next step of our plan. Somewhere on the island waited Anthony Dunkin, which meant an ending I'd been looking for for a long time was about to happen.

Jayson Hernandez at my side, looking as adorable and kissable as I'd ever seen him.

My biological father, on the near horizon.

The cold-hearted woman who spurned my new friend.

A spectacular Caribbean getaway in an unprecedented way where I knew absolutely no one.

This wedding would be one for the record books.

Chapter Eight

JAYSON

A wall of warmth met me the moment I exited the puddle-jumper airplane that I had feared would kill us. Dagny and I stepped off our third plane hours later and into a glimmering world of sun, sand, and sky. Dagny grinned, her head tilted back and eyes closed.

Sunlight warmed my face and neck as the pilot stepped off the plane and gestured toward a golf cart not far away. A familiar, athletic body climbed out of the cart and moved toward us with a pearlescent smile. He wore a bright floral shirt and a pair of khaki shorts with flip flops.

"There's the hideous groom," I called.

Grady slammed into me with the force of two colliding titans, unmistakable with his coiled black hair and ultra-white teeth. We chest-thumped and back-pounded for a few moments, then pulled away laughing.

Grady glanced back, saw Dagny there, and smiled warmly.

"Hey Dagny."

She shuffled forward, her arms at her side as a quick smile brightened her face. "Hi G-grady. Good to s-s-see you again."

Again?

She stuck out her hand but he wrapped her in a long embrace that lasted at least twenty minutes too long.

"You have a fiancée, you dog," I muttered, and Grady laughed. The wind fluttered Dagny's hair off her shoulder as he pulled away, but she looked ready to curl up there all day long. Yeah, not happening. Not with Grady. Nor Vik. Definitely not Bastian. I yanked her back.

"Thank you for coming with this knucklehead." Grady winked at her. "We can't dress him up or take him anywhere."

I slammed a good-natured fist into his shoulder, but Grady laughed it off and reached for Dagny's bag, which the pilot had unloaded behind us.

"Come on," Grady said. "Your shared bungalow is all ready and Vikram's already here, looking for the wet bar and the closest single woman."

"He's probably half drunk by now."

"We can only be so lucky."

Dagny followed just behind me, her head whipping around to take the place in, while Grady rambled about the wedding party, new arrivals, and Helene's obsession with adhering to traditional wedding rules like a best man speech, something that gave me no fear. Public speaking? I got this.

In the golf cart, we cruised away from the small landing strip and over to a hotel plunked in the middle of an island. Coconut trees stretched high overhead and cast long shadows as the sun sank toward a crystal-blue horizon. A distant storm slanted across the far edge sky, but the rest of it was a clear, cerulean blue.

People dotted the beach here and there, but the white sand was largely quiet. White-capped waves made me want to plunge right in under the hot sun. My thoughts drifted to Dagny in a swimming suit, and I had to reel that line of thought back in real quick. The whole place was small enough we could drive the perimeter in two hours, I'd guess.

The warm air, bright sunshine, and gentle whisper of the surf made me itch to get in the water already.

Out of the corner of my eye, I could see the wind whipping Dagny's hair out of her face and across her eyes in a charming dance. Her lips were turned slightly up in a half-smile as she ran her gaze over the shrubby trees and sandy path that led to the hotel. A far cry from the usual view at the Frolicking Moose, for sure. I wanted to watch her soak it up, like experiencing the world from a whole new lens.

"Bastian is flying in tonight," Grady said as the golf cart plunked onto a blacktop path. The whine of the engine carried us closer to a small, circular bungalow set away from the hotel. A wooden porch ringed it, and grasses jutted off the top in a charming island display. "Won't be here until later. I tried to get you separate rooms, but they're all booked out with Helene's family. She's got a ton of the hotel, if not the whole damned thing. For an island getaway, it's not that big." Grady glanced in the rearview mirror. "I did, however, manage to move things around so the two of you got a bungalow with separate rooms. You can have it to yourself, Dagny, if you want. Jayson can bunk outside, with Bastian."

"Outside?" she asked.

I smirked and said over my shoulder, "Bastian prefers to sleep in the open air."

"He's bringing a hammock," Grady said, as if that explained everything. To Dagny's credit, she shrugged.

"S-sounds fun."

That didn't leave the little matter of sharing the bungalow settled, but we could figure that out later. With weather like this, a hammock would be a dream. Grady stopped the golf cart after a ten minute ride, not far from the beach. A figure with a floppy hat and a light green dress stepped out of the bungalow as we approached. Grady grinned the sparkling smile that captured most women.

"There she is," he murmured quietly, and bounded out of the golf cart with his too-large body. Seconds later, Helene let out a little cry as he swept her up and nuzzled her neck.

"S-so sweet," Dagny said.

"So nauseating," I quipped with a little wink, then stepped out of the golf cart. Dagny followed before I could offer to help. She reached for her bag, but I got there first. Apparently, she wasn't going to make this easy. Even if I wasn't sure what *this* was.

She smiled. "Th-thanks."

"Anytime."

Her head tilted back to study the wooden house covered with a grass-thatch roof that sloped down just above my head. White lights draped the outside, already glowing. The smell of bacon drifted through the air from what appeared to be a gathering below. A few open doors and windows gave us a quick peek inside a spacious, mostly wooden interior. Beyond that lay the beach, studded with tiki torches and hotel staff wearing the same uniform.

Dagny ignored all of that and smiled curiously at Helene, who was tucked into Grady's side. Dagny's expression was serene, but something about it didn't seem right. Her arms were a little too rigid at her side. Her face, a little *too* neutral. Was she intimidated by Helene? Most would be, considering the family Helene had.

"It's w-wonderful to meet you, H-helene," Dagny murmured. "C-congratulations on the w-wedding and thank you f-for letting me be p-part of it."

A moment of surprise registered in Helene's honey-colored eyes, then she smiled. "Thank you for coming! It's Dagny, right? We're so excited to have you." Her gaze darted to mine with another warm grin. "It's been far too long since Hernandez extracted himself from his deputy cruiser to come and play with us."

I wrapped Helene in a warm hug that earned a glare from Grady two seconds before he pulled her back.

"Long enough," he muttered with a growl of warning. I laughed.

"Please, ignore my caveman fiancé and come inside." Helene gestured to the bungalow with a wave. "I'm sorry we don't have separate living spaces for you. Most of my family has taken up the hotel because Grady's family preferred the bungalows. This one does have two rooms and a common area. I hope that's okay?"

Fine by me, I wanted to say, but let Dagny respond first.

"Yes, of c-course. Th-thank you."

Helene smiled and drew Dagny farther into the open room, which had a kitchen on the right. She left me and Grady behind. Grady stopped and glanced at me out of the corner of his eyes. I set Dagny's bag aside.

"I like her."

I rolled my eyes. "You've said five words to her. And it doesn't matter anyway," I added. "She's just helping me out because of Victoria."

He shrugged. "I like her. It's weird to see her here, though, of all places. And with someone so far below her league it isn't even funny. Does she still work at the Diner?"

Grady and his family left Pineville as soon as he graduated high school, and only returned when Vik and I pulled him back with a new, treacherous alpine climb or a white water rafting trip during the summer. For him to know anything about Pineville startled me.

"Not anymore," I said.

He shook his head. "She's grown up a lot."

"What are you talking about?"

Grady tilted his head toward her. "Dagny Taylor, right? She went to school with us."

"Shut up."

He rolled his eyes. "Man, you have always been *so* blind. She was younger, but definitely in high school. I remember her stutter. She didn't say much. I think we took auto tech together."

Dagny taking auto didn't surprise me much. The wooden pallet furniture made it clear she was a woman that loved to piece things together and work with her hands. But Grady knowing her from school threw me for a loop. He couldn't be serious. If Dagny went to school with us, I would have remembered.

Or . . . maybe not.

Bonehead was the best description for me during that time of my life. Her amused response to Grady's mother setting me up with every bridesmaid on the island suddenly made a lot more sense. Plus, Grady had a mind like a steel trap. If he remembered her, then so it was.

Weird.

All this time, Dagny had known me better than I knew her. Something about that made me uneasy. What had I missed all these years? Dagny had been around . . . always. How had I not noticed her?

Grady clapped me on the shoulder. "Now that you've thoroughly embarrassed yourself, I can't wait to hear how it goes when you confess you didn't remember her. Hey, did you see Victoria yet?"

"No."

He clucked. "Good luck, man. She's on the prowl."

"For me?"

His eyes widened. "For a man. Her date ditched and she doesn't like being anywhere alone." He glanced to his watch, sighed, and called, "Hey baby. We better get going. We have to meet up with the coordinator about the dinner, remember?"

Helene turned, the picture of grace, and stepped up to his side with a smile so warm I would have assumed they'd been separated for weeks. Grady put an arm around her waist, and, watching the two of them, I couldn't remember why Vikram protested relationships so much.

"See you in an hour?" Helene asked me.

I nodded. "We'll be there."

"Right on the beach." Grady stepped back, his fingers entwined with Helene's. "Open seating and bar, so we'll see you there. Oh, and take a shower, dude. You stink."

* * *

Any news of Victoria shook me up, but knowing she was on the hunt made it even worse.

In my very fortunate life, I'd survived avalanches, cliff jumping, and a really stupid stunt where I rode a crappy old rug down a church steeple, but I'd also been a deputy for almost ten years. Despite all that life experience, Victoria still scared the crap out of me.

There was something unnerving about the subterfuge that lay behind her thick veneer of courtesy and sincerity. Really, she wasn't sincere. But somehow, she managed to make herself *feel* sincere.

Once Helene and Grady left, I sniffed my shirt. Did I really stink? Probably. Planes never smelled good. The fresh air blowing in distracted me from thoughts of a shower, however. When I looked up to see Dagny standing at the edge of the balcony, everything disappeared from my brain except for her. She had a way of doing that. Whether it was the casual way her body leaned into the wind, the delighted smile on her face, or the quiet way she seemed to watch everything. Her brown hair fluttered behind her again, and I had to crush another wave of attraction. It drew my thoughts back to what Grady said.

How could I have *not* noticed her in high school?

Beyond her glittered the sapphire ocean, ringed in turquoise around a perfect beach that called to me.

Forget the shower.

Dagny and I needed to talk.

Dagny glanced over with a warm smile when I stepped up next to her, careful to keep a foot of distance between us. When her gaze returned to the ocean, I noticed a line in her forehead that hadn't been there before. She seemed . . . distracted. Maybe just deep in thought. For several minutes, we stood in the breeze off the water and I tried to imagine another time when I'd seen something so perfectly calm.

"So," I drawled. "You went to high school with us?"

Her lips twitched with a suppressed smile, but she didn't look my way. "Y-you're just remembering?"

I snorted. "No. I don't remember you at all."

She laughed. "I w-wasn't exactly memorable. N-not compared to the Merry Idiots."

I almost choked. There had been a small hope that she *hadn't* known me as a Merry Idiot, but that was a long shot anyway. Man, were we knuckleheads in high school if someone like Dagny knew about us. My thoughts traveled to our legendary C-tape with a little shudder. Once upon a time, I'd been exorbitantly proud of it. Now? The jury was still out.

Hopefully she *never* saw that.

"You couldn't have been a senior with me," I said as I dove deeper into my memories and tried to find her there. "I would remember that. I think."

"F-f-freshman." Her gaze drifted to mine for a second and then back. Whatever trouble had occluded her gaze from before had now cleared, like a storm blowing out of the sky. "You have no r-r-reason to remember me. G-grady remembered me, I im-magine?"

"Yeah."

Even though she'd exonerated my name from not remembering her, I still felt sheepish. Our high school educated kids from both little Pineville and the slightly-bigger-but-not-that-much-bigger Jackson City. Mountain towns weren't exactly population centers. Our school map covered so many miles it could take over an hour to drive to another kid's house. Plus, I had a feeling Dagny had always lived quietly.

"Auto t-t-tech?" she asked. "D-did he remember me from a-auto?"

I nodded. She laughed and pushed a strand of hair away from her face. Whether it was the bright sunshine, the diamond-like sparkle of the water, or just the shedding of stress and life that came with vacation, she seemed like a whole new person here. Glowing, in fact.

Damn beautiful, too.

For a moment, I tried to picture her in the Diner and the Frolicking Moose, with her casual bun held up by pens and the jeans that dragged a little by her heels, as if she didn't want to bother with cutting them. Such a relaxed picture, transposed against such rampant island beauty, still seemed just as honest.

In other words, Dagny could fit anywhere.

"Yeah," I croaked. "Auto."

She laughed harder. "One d-d-day, Grady smashed his f-fingers in the hood of a C-corvette." Her words turned into a giggle, then a rolling laugh. "H-he squealed a-a-and another kid d-dropped an oil pan. Our teacher s-slipped on the oil and h-hit his head j-just as the principal walked in. W-would have b-been okay, except he said the F word in f-f-front of all of us *and* the p-p-principal."

Tears slipped out of the corner of her eyes as she kept laughing. The infectious sound caught me, and I chuckled with the thought of Grady's high-pitched squeal. Same one he'd let out when we bought a crab from the grocery store deli and he let it bite his nipple on a dare.

"I know the exact squeal," I said.

She wiped off the tears and her laugh slowed. "It w-was unf-f-forgettable."

"Why didn't you tell me?" I turned to lean my back against the railing. "All this time we've seen each other in Pineville and you never mentioned it."

My pride was far too macho to admit it, but I felt a bit put-out that she'd keep such a detail quiet. Why didn't she mention it before? That kind of detail connected people, and maybe if I'd *connected* with Dagny sooner, I wouldn't feel so rummy over her now.

Dagny's smile widened even as a hint of a blush rose to her cheeks.

"You n-never asked."

At that, I laughed. "You're right. I should have started a conversation with, 'Hey, just want to clear up the off chance that we ever went to high school together?'"

Her laugh bubbled back up again, a clear song against the backdrop of waves. "Exactly. Th-this is all y-your fault."

"I take full responsibility."

Her amusement faded slightly. She leaned both hands on the railings, let out a long breath, and smiled at nothing. When the breeze stroked her cheeks, she closed her eyes and let her hair dance around her face.

I looked away and cleared my throat.

"So, what did you think of Helene?" I asked.

The muscles along the back of her neck tightened a little, but released when she let out a long breath. Her voice was bright. Perhaps a little too bright.

"V-very sweet."

"This is only my second time meeting her," I said, "but she's always left a good impression whenever she catches me on the phone or a video chat with Grady. Grady loves her, which is saying something."

"I-I had no trouble s-speaking to her."

"Do you struggle speaking to people?"

She tilted her head to the side, then nodded. "Y-yeah. If I'm n-nervous or tense it gets worse. B-but it's not as bad w-when I'm w-with people I'm c-comfortable with."

"That's good to know."

A calm stretch of silence fell between us next. After the rush of airports, plane switches, and trying not to think too far ahead to worry over Victoria, the quiet was a balm. Dagny leaned forward, her head canted slightly to the side.

"Th-thank you for b-bringing me. Even if th-this is all I s-s-saw, it would be worth it."

My thoughts drifted to Victoria for just a moment, then I forced it away. Victoria looked like a black hole compared to Dagny's natural luminescence. Between them, there was no competition.

"I owe you big time for coming," I said wryly. "And don't get too ahead of yourself yet. The fun has just begun."

My tone must have given me away because she turned to look at me in concern. "V-victoria?"

"She'll be at the dinner tonight. Grady said her date stood her up and she's on the prowl for another one. She doesn't strike me as the type that likes being thwarted."

Dagny smiled with one side of her lips. "Th-that's f-fine." She held out a hand, fingers splayed. I hesitated only a moment, then slipped my hand in hers. "W-we'll f-face her together."

My fingers squeezed hers. Victoria might make an appearance at the dinner, but that didn't mean I had to talk to her. For now, I was content to avoid Victoria, and enjoy Dagny.

To me, that was the best plan yet.

"Then let's get ready," I said with a little smile and wondered if she heard my relief. "That island barbecue isn't going to eat itself."

Chapter Nine

DAGNY

The sound of the shower across the bungalow stopped just as I slipped into my own bathroom.

Bright lights illuminated a petite bathroom with sparkling white tile floors and a green potted plant with fronds sprouting out of it, tucked away in the corner. I set my toiletry bag on a glittering black bathroom counter and released a breath that felt as if it had been trapped in my lungs for days. When I stared into the mirror, bags seemed to have already collected under my eyes.

I tore my gaze away, cranked the shower onto its hottest setting, and stripped out of my airplane-grubby clothes. The smell of Jayson's soap drifted through the door and swirled through my nose until I ripped open one of the bars the hotel provided and passed it under my face just to distract me. A tropical, coconut scent followed, momentarily erasing him from my thoughts.

Yes, I thought. *Go away, Jayson. You and your adorable friendship with Grady. Your warm affection for Helene. The way you smiled at strangers and accidentally touched my leg earlier on the plane. Go. Away.*

The hot water eased some of the tense knots in my shoulders as I replayed the plane ride, the arrival, and finally my short, quick visit with Helene. Sweet, lovely Helene.

My half-sister.

Did lineage count if your family didn't know you existed? Were siblings siblings by virtue of DNA alone? Growing up as an only child had always left me thirsty for outside connections. For anyone but just me in the house, in my life. Someone to lean back on. A tie to another soul that only came from something like life together. Helene was the closest thing I would ever have to that, and she had no idea who I was.

Water cascaded over my shoulders, sending away the grime and sweat of the airport as I lathered my hair into a wet mess of coconut. My thoughts traveled to Grady, my conversation with Jayson that still brought a smile to my face, and finally to the upcoming dinner.

Would Anthony be there?

I sincerely hoped not. At least, not yet. I needed a little more time and a good night's sleep to settle into this strange reality. The wedding was still two days away, which meant Anthony could be away from the island. Unlikely, considering the crowd that gathered on the beach outside our bungalow after Helene and Grady left. For a moment, I thought about checking in with Serafina, but held back. She didn't know about Anthony and would only want Jayson details.

No, I wanted to see this through on my own.

Water sluiced down my back as I scrubbed the shampoo out of my hair, slicked conditioner in after it, and mentally reviewed my plan of attack. How to *not* embarrass Jayson. What to wear. Mentally preparing myself for meeting a room of total strangers always required time, silence, and a lot of girl power statements.

Talking to strangers wasn't as daunting as the thought of sitting with Jayson through a dinner where some crazy woman might give me the stink eye, all while he would smell impossibly good. Victoria had nothing to do with my trepidation. I'd doubtless conquered worse at the coffee shop or Diner. But if he kept shooting that smile my way?

Well, there'd be no pretending affection on my part.

I had a few stutter-free cards up my sleeve that I only used when I absolutely had to. Tonight called for it. *I got this,* I told myself. *Too easy.*

But I wasn't sure whether I meant the dinner, or keeping Jayson at bay from my too-large heart.

* * *

Thirty minutes later, I slipped out of the bathroom in a bright yellow and pink sundress, a pair of flip flops with subtle, sparkling yellow diamonds along the edges, and my hair straightened around my face. Makeup wasn't part of my daily repertoire at the coffee shop, but I slipped some mascara and lip gloss on.

Jayson's voice stopped me halfway across the wooden floor. I paused, my dirty clothes tucked under one arm, to see a pair of flip flops on his feet. My gaze slowly traveled higher, past sculpted calves, cargo shorts, up to a tapered waist and a subtle, short-sleeved sky-blue button-up that highlighted his dark skin and broad shoulders. I stopped at his lips, unable to look higher.

"Wow," he whispered. "Damn, Dagny."

My breath caught the moment I had the courage to look in his eyes. The tangy scent of his soap—which my brain only registered as *man smell*— swirled in my head until I could barely think. He'd left the stubble on his cheeks. His thick, short hair was just a little tousled and still slightly wet.

"You l-l-look great," I said.

He whistled. "So. Do. You."

"Thanks."

He trapped my gaze again, blinked, and then turned around as if he'd forgotten something. "I, uh . . . " He cleared his throat. "Are you ready to go? Where are we going again? Oh! The beach. Right. Yes. Are you ready?"

Startled back to myself, I shook my head and headed for my room, which was tucked back out of the way.

"Yeah, l-let m-m-me just p-put this away."

Once in my room, I set my dirty clothes aside, stopped, and drew in a deep breath. Panicked butterflies filled my chest now. What was I thinking? No way could I do this. No way could I attend this dinner and impress his friends and frighten off his ex-almost-girlfriend and *not* fall in love with him in the process.

Get it together, I said with a mental slap. *Get. It. Together.*

With the sinking feeling of a deepening attraction sitting like a pit in my stomach, I reached for my purse, then realized I didn't need one. On a last minute decision, I left my phone tucked in my backpack. No accoutrements tonight. The sensation of not carrying my phone with me left me feeling naked when I stepped back out. Jayson stopped, looked at me one more time, and held out a bent arm. His eyes held a silent question.

"R-ready," I said, then slipped my arm through his.

He pulled me closer, tucked my arm into his side, and led us out. My heart pattered with his warmth so close to my skin, and I wanted to pull myself all the way into him. Wanted the heavy weight of his arm around my waist instead of tucked up against my ribcage. I forced my mind to turn from these thoughts. They would do me no favors tonight.

The sun had left the horizon in a wash of magenta as we stepped onto the sand. He guided us away from the beach house toward an open stretch of sand where tiki torches burned bright around a banquet table of food. Servers scuttled around, busily carting food, wine, and what appeared to be champagne. The smell of pineapple and pork lay heavy on the air amongst piles of rice, fish, and several elegant sushi rolls.

Couples mingled throughout torch-lit sand as we approached. In the middle of them stood Grady and Helene, laughing. Grady kept his arm lovingly around her. Helene appeared to be introducing him to a family member, because she kissed an older woman on the cheek, then gestured to Grady. My eyes didn't stray from that older couple. Who were they? How did she know them? Were they also related to me? Although I studied every person I could see, none of them were clearly Anthony Dunkin.

A weird sort of relief followed.

"There are more people than I expected," Jayson said quietly. He kept us along the edge of the crowd, steering us toward round tables where candles danced in the gentle breeze. His arm had tensed slightly under my hand. The surf lingered not far away, a constant hum of activity in the background.

"It's a l-lovely d-d-dinner," I agreed as he led me to a table so far back, none others were behind us. The ring of light from the torches extended just to where we sat, but not beyond. He glanced around with a quick smile to someone that called to him. Although he seemed at ease enough, there was a current of tension in the way he held his jaw. The relentless searching of his gaze.

"H-have you s-spotted her yet?" I asked quietly as my arm slipped away from his. He didn't seem to notice me take a step back, closer to the table where I could breathe a little better.

"Yes."

I let my eyes wander the growing crowd to see if I could pick her out without being obvious. More people meandered down sandy paths toward the beach. The house where we were staying wasn't far from here, buttery warm lights illuminating it in the darkening sky.

"Where?" I asked.

"Twelve o'clock. Red dress, no shoes, at the bar."

By the time my eyes naturally wandered there, a crowd of people that had been waiting for drinks had dispersed. Two people remained. One, a stoop-backed male with dusty gray hair. The other a female with glossy legs that stretched into forever and a stunning dress that would have made a rose jealous. Black hair that danced across her shoulders in gentle waves, sculpted cheeks, and a coy smile caught my attention. I looked away before Victoria caught my gaze.

"I don't think she's seen me yet."

"W-what if you j-just got this over w-with?" I asked. "Talk to her. M-maybe she'll ignore y-you after that."

Jayson frowned. "Maybe." But I could tell that my suggestion was as likely as rain in this pristine night sky. Stars popped out overhead. A waiter slipped by, then stopped and held a tray in my direction.

"Wine?"

Not wanting to dull my brain, or make my thoughts less clear so my stutter grew worse, I waved it off with a warm smile. "N-no. Th-thank you."

We lingered at the table for a few moments while Jayson seemed to pull himself back together. Then a call came from a few steps away, and Jayson looked over. A grin spread across his face seconds before a meaty male tackled him into a hug. They collapsed into the sand, laughing.

Meanwhile, a pair of eyes met mine through the flickering light of the tiki torches.

Victoria stared hard at me, her expression more curious than hostile. Still, it sent a cold feeling through my veins like an ice bath. I met her gaze, too startled to look away. Beneath layers of curiosity in that stare, I sensed something big.

She tilted her head and motioned out toward the waves,

where the light stopped behind the torches and the waves hissed. A quiet invitation. I glanced around to confirm that I didn't imagine her asking me, but no one else stood at my back. Jayson spoke with his football-player sized friend a few tables away, laughing uproariously at something the other one said.

Victoria lifted an eyebrow in question. Or was it a challenge?

I nodded.

Then followed her out into the sandy darkness.

* * *

"I'm Victoria."

We met several yards away from the dinner party, beyond where the light of the torches reached, near the surf. Wedding guests trapped in the glowing overhead lights, tiki torches, and fast, staccatos of laughter lingered at our backs. She held out a hand and I accepted it. Her handshake was firm, quick, and she released me a second later.

"Dagny."

The word flowed without a stutter by sheer luck. Water hissed around my feet where we stopped at the surf.

Victoria smiled. "It's good to meet you."

Is it? I wanted to ask, but kept the question at bay. Beneath her smile, she did seem curious. Maybe even sincere. But who was I to Jayson except a friend? The same thing that she should be, except I wasn't sure anymore. His reaction to her had been suspiciously strong. Did he still have feelings for her? My gut clenched just thinking about it.

Besides, why would my presence with Jayson prompt her to want a conversation with me? Lingering emotions, probably. She wasn't over Jayson either? Maybe they'd rekindle whatever they had before and come back together. Wouldn't that be the worst trip ever?

Then again, she might be jealous of competition. Although the thought of *me* being competition almost made me laugh.

There was no tension in Victoria's perfectly sculpted shoulders, no annoyance in her words. Maybe she'd moved on and forgotten him. For all I knew, a new man waited on the other side of the dinner table with a plate for each of them, but I doubted it. No one beckoned another woman away from a guy like Jayson just to be friends.

She turned her face to the gentle breeze off the ocean and closed her eyes in the exact same pose that captured me an hour before.

"It's perfect here, isn't it?" she asked.

"Yes," I said, but my voice was a quiet singsong. Turning words into subtle, quiet melodies removed the stutter. It could be an awkward way to speak, requiring more attention to my words than ever, but it got me through the most important conversations without stumbling all over myself. For some reason, this conversation seemed to merit such work more than any others I could recall.

"Helene has always had wonderful taste," Victoria said. "An island getaway wedding just . . . fits her. So does Grady." She laughed quietly to herself. "He's good for her. She needs him and his . . . grounding influence."

I laughed incredulously and she turned to me with a questioning smile.

"Is Grady not grounding?" she asked.

"Oh, I don't know. Maybe. He was a very wild teenager. That's why I laughed."

She tilted her head to the side, then smiled. "Yes, that makes sense."

"To think of him as *grounding* is . . . a-amusing." The stutter that slipped didn't seem to catch her attention yet, but my throat tightened at the thought. In some ways, the singsong and hope of sounding normal felt ingenuine. Would I always have to speak this way in front of her? Was the stutter something to hide?

I shoved aside those questions.

"I suppose we all change," she mused quietly.

While the stars popped out overhead and the water tickled my toes, I wondered if Jayson was looking for me yet. Would he be stressed? What would he think if he found me here with Victoria, of all people?

Why did she ask me to come?

Her easygoing greeting, even the calm conversation, hadn't disarmed me at all. While I didn't think of her as a wild woman bent on hunting down a man, I couldn't discount that sometimes the most frightening monsters had the brightest smiles. Still, this whole trip suddenly made less sense and I didn't know how to reorient.

Seconds after the thoughts filtered back out of my mind, Victoria let out a long breath. "You're here with Jayson?" she asked. In her wavering voice was a hint of vulnerability that had to be at least a little authentic.

"Yes."

"Ah."

The word was swept into the ocean breeze, and I let the silence lay between us because I didn't know what to say. Only the milling sound of the growing dinner crowd filtered through, with an occasional loud laugh thrown in for emphasis.

"He's spoken about me to you, I would imagine," she murmured.

"A f-few things, yes."

She glanced at me from the corner of her smoky eyes, but whether it was regarding the stutter or what I said, I wasn't sure.

"That I was a monster, perhaps?"

The surprise in my tone was sincere. "N-no."

She chuckled, as if amused, but the lightness had fallen out of her tone. "What has he told you?"

"He s-said you had a f-falling out and the r-relationship died before it b-began, that's all."

The gentle summation of their odd experience felt incomplete and filled with holes, like Swiss cheese. Neither Jayson nor Victoria were *monsters*, yet I didn't want her to have a reason to make him into one. If I relayed all the details he'd told me, I had no doubt she'd use it against him somehow.

Victoria's expression didn't change as she absorbed what I said, her jaw highlighted by the lights behind us.

"Falling out," she murmured. "How . . . interesting."

I straightened. Time to end this on a good note or before it dove too deep. Besides, I was honest enough with myself to admit that I didn't want to know if she was fishing for information. Maybe she came to decide if I was competition or not, and then she'd make her move when she had the truth.

That would be utterly unbearable.

"D-do you n-need something from me?" I asked. "I d-didn't tell him where I was going and I don't want him to be worried."

"He is the kind sort, isn't he?"

I nodded.

"An introduction was all." She turned to me with that warm smile yet again. Facing me fully, and only an arm's length away, she was more stunning than ever. Starlight seemed to add an aura of mystery to her dark eyes. Her expression softened a little, smudged with concern. "And . . . perhaps a gentle warning for your sake."

"W-warning?"

"One that I wished someone had given me when Jayson and I . . . when we crossed paths. We may have only been together for a week or so but, my goodness, did it feel so much longer than that."

All my attention focused on the effort to maintain an impartial expression. My eyebrows lifted slightly in a sign of encouragement, and she took it.

"Jayson is a wonderful person. At least, that's my assumption. I can't say that I know him well after things didn't work out between us."

"When you told him he wouldn't make enough money for you to be happy?"

The question wasn't meant to be a jab. At least, not a conscious one. But the darkening of her eyes told me that's exactly how she took it. Still, I couldn't help but feel for her. I had been on the losing end of Jayson Hernandez my whole life. Wanting what one couldn't have was the worst kind of torture, particularly when he was involved. The man could be so clueless sometimes.

Victoria laughed mirthlessly, one arm crossed across her middle to hold the other. "Yes, I imagine that is how he paraphrased what I said, although it's not at all what was intended. I would never hurt him."

Her tone became breathless. She blinked several times and cleared her throat. When she tucked a strand of hair behind her ears, it shifted back out in the breeze, but she didn't seem to notice. Instead, she seemed a million miles away.

"If he wants to make what we had smaller than it was," she added quickly and with a pained expression, "then let him. I've endured worse; I imagine I can take that as well. We all deal with grief and loss in our own ways. But you deserve the truth, at least. I'll sleep better at night if you've had the warning."

A haunted expression crossed her face. She frowned, lips pouted, the picture of grief in her beautiful feminine state. Even my mind, so loyal to a man that barely knew I existed, began to wonder.

Did Jayson tell me the truth?

What details didn't I have? At this point, I just needed to leave. Warning or not, I didn't need to hear it.

"Th-thank you for introducing yourself," I said. "I hope you enjoy the wedding and this b-beautiful n-night."

She pulled her eyebrows up. "You don't want to hear it?"

"N-no, thank you."

She blinked several times. Her mouth opened, closed, then opened again when she said, "Very well. Have a good night. Tell Jayson I would . . . I'd love to see him."

She trailed off, and I didn't doubt what she said. Nor could I entirely disregard what she'd revealed. Almost a decade of reverential-like worship, and Jayson had only just realized I existed. Only an idiot *wouldn't* see my adoration for him.

An idiot named Jayson Hernandez.

With the party a few steps away and Jayson surely looking for me now, I didn't fear Victoria yet. What would she do, smack me with her shoe? But the edge of something in her eyes was unsettling, and I had a feeling I could only see a minuscule part of whatever she harbored in that quick, manipulative mind.

"G-good night."

She opened her mouth to say something, but her gaze caught on something over my shoulder. I felt someone standing back there, but didn't dare turn around. Victoria's upper lip curled slightly, then she issued an almost-warm smile to whoever stood back there.

"The conquering hero returns," she murmured.

"Back to your hole, snake," muttered a deep voice behind me.

Victoria sent a cold glare back there, looked at me with a quick nod of farewell, then filtered back to the circle of light. I spun around to find a towering man a few steps away. He wore flip flops, a pack high on one shoulder, and an old gray t-shirt that flapped in the wind. Tousled, sandy hair gave way to bright blue eyes and a golden beard that shimmered in the low light. He stood in the shadows like a hulking god, and the slightest hint of smoke curled off him.

"Hello B-bastian," I whispered.

"Dagny."

He studied me for a moment and I wondered if he remembered me. He must have, because didn't he just use my name? Of all the Merry Idiots, Bastian had always been the quietest. The thinker. It had been Bastian holed up in the closet of the library the day I was able to see the whole C-tape. He knew where the old VHS was stored and showed the movie to a few friends when I stumbled onto them. I'd intentionally kept quiet, deterred a librarian, and he'd later thanked me for not ratting them out.

But would he remember that quiet girl who volunteered in the library? Or did he just know me as the girl who made his coffee?

He motioned to the circle of lights with a nod. "Jay's looking for you. Go ahead. I'll keep an eye on her."

"Y-you think sh-she'd hurt me?"

"Never turn your back on Victoria Haynes."

With that unnerving thought, I glanced back into the light where the dinner party continued. Victoria lingered near the edge of the light, but kept her back to us. The strange thought that she hadn't asked if Jayson and I were dating filtered through my mind. She'd clearly made an assumption—a fair one—about our relationship status.

Everything had changed now that I'd met her.

I could change with it.

Victoria's attempt to turn me against Jayson by telling me whatever lie she had only made me want to lace my shoes on tighter. There was no one else more prepared to act madly in love with Jayson Hernandez than me because it wouldn't be an act. Despite her calm veneer, I sensed that Victoria still had her eye on Jayson.

She wasn't about to stop her chase.

All I had to do to help him was everything I'd dreamed of doing with Jayson for the last ten years. Laugh with him. Joke with him. Be so close I could smell him all the way in my sleep. Being his *girlfriend* could provide some level of protection against Victoria so he could enjoy the break and the time with his friends.

You against me, Victoria, I thought. *He will never be yours again.*

I might lose my heart in the process, but at least it would break for the man I'd always loved.

JAYSON

There was no reason to panic, but I couldn't help the way my chest tightened.

Where. Was. Dagny?

Every woman that walked by and wasn't her or Victoria sent me into another little spiral. Had Victoria found her? Had she run off for some reason? I kept an easy expression on my face and a beer in hand as I skirted the edge of the party. Sand slipped through my toes. Waves crashed. People laughed. My heart sped up even as I tried to calm it down. We were on a literal island—there was nowhere for her to go that I couldn't find.

Aside from that massive ocean.

Thoughts of Victoria so close by were not reassuring.

Regret for not immediately introducing Dagny to my friend Jameson, and then pulling her to my side to keep her anchored near, kept me on high alert. Maybe Victoria got to her. Maybe Dagny didn't want to be here. When a warm hand touched my back, right between my shoulder blades, I whipped around.

Dagny stood there, color high on her cheeks despite the perfect temperature. She smiled, slipped closer, and slid an arm around my waist. My heart thudded in my chest as she pressed her cheek to mine and whispered, "Play along?"

With a little encouragement from her, my hand slid around her waist. Instinctively, I pulled her closer, but there wasn't far for her to go. My thoughts only extended as far as the heat of her breath on the sensitive part of my neck, right below my earlobe.

Play along?

"V-victoria and I just m-m-met," she said quietly, so only I could hear.

My arm tightened around her, but before I could demand an answer, she kept speaking. This time without stuttering, her voice a smooth melody.

"Everything is fine, but I think Grady was wise to warn you. She's on your path. I think, for your sake, we retract my plan and move to yours, *boyfriend*."

Like it had a will of its own, my other arm wrapped around her. Her breath escaped her in a little gasp of surprise when I tightened her against me, her chest pressing into mine. The hitch of her breath against my neck sent my stomach into a tailspin. I only vaguely wondered how she spoke without breaking the words apart. My mind was too occupied with the feeling of her smooth dress against the palms of my hands.

"You okay?" I whispered.

"Fine," she murmured brightly. "Victoria doesn't frighten me, nor does she fool me."

Relief followed her statement like the flash of heat from a shot of whiskey. Had I been worried that Dagny would believe Victoria? The thought was insulting, but I couldn't dismiss it. The tips of her fingers played with the hair along the back of my neck and scattered my thoughts like breaking glass. After this, my heart would never be the same.

Shadows moved behind Dagny. I glanced up to see Bastian standing a few steps away, his travel backpack slung over his shoulder. He held a small laptop in one hand, the same one he carried everywhere, but no one knew what he did with it. He jerked his head in greeting and I returned it. My gaze trailed back to his bag.

"You brought it?" I mouthed, then gestured to the bag. He grinned and gave me a thumbs up.

"Taken care of, boss," he said quietly.

Operation Prank Out the Groom was on its way.

"Remember," Dagny whispered, oblivious to our conversation as she pulled away from my too-close embrace, "we're l-l-lovers now, not f-f-friends."

As if I needed help pretending to be stunned by her.

Bastian stepped up, slapped my back in a man hug, and muttered, "Saw the whole thing. Talk later."

When I returned to Dagny, I put my arm around her shoulders and kept her tight to my side. I didn't like that any interaction happened between her and Victoria that I'd missed, but at least Bastian had been there. Victoria was too much of an unknown, and Dagny wasn't safe with her alone.

Dagny glanced at the food table as my stomach gurgled. She laughed and patted my stomach.

"Let's f-f-feed that b-beast."

Bastian growled and dropped his pack into the sand with a thud.

"Food."

Fifteen minutes later, we sat at the table. Bastian wolfed down food while I kept an eye on the bar for Vikram. Dagny didn't require much conversation, and I was too preoccupied trying to calm my instincts. Crowds. Alcohol. Beaches. Fire. All of it added up to an interesting cocktail of danger that could explode at any moment.

Not on duty, I reminded myself. *Not in charge here.*

Didn't matter, I felt on high alert anyway.

Dagny put a hand on my arm and pulled me out a spiral of thought. I blinked and looked over, wondering if I slid so far into memories or possibilities that I'd missed something she said. Was I ignoring her? This was exactly why I didn't date. Because my attention was always *everywhere.*

She held a piece of pineapple between two fingers.

"T-try it. It's gr-r-rilled."

My lips parted to say something, but my brain stalled again. She sat beneath the light of a nearby tiki torch, and shadows flickered over her skin, turning it a golden shade. With a charming, quick smile, she held the fruit closer. A teasing expression followed with a dash of challenge.

"S-scared?"

In one quick move, I grabbed the whole piece, then sucked the sweet juice off her fingers. Her eyes widened but she didn't retract her hand. Instead, she smiled wider, dropped her hand, then leaned back. As if this were the most natural state in the world for her. As if we'd always done this. That was something I could get used to. Dagny at my side. *Flirty* Dagny at my side, teasing me with that smile and fruit.

Why *hadn't* we done this?

Bastian stared at us, one eyebrow lifted.

"How was the flight, Sebastian?" I asked, just to wipe that look of contemplation out of his eyes.

"Call me Sebastian again," he muttered, "and I'll run a kabob through your pretty eyes, Hernandez."

Riling him up always made me feel better. I laughed as he chugged half a glass of ice water.

"You missing any good fires?"

"A 100,000 acre inferno in Nevada." He crunched some ice between his back teeth, then lounged back. "So . . . not really."

"The h-hot s-sun here must be just w-what you want during the m-middle of fire season," Dagny quipped. Bastian's lips twitched. He glanced behind him, where the ocean crashed, and set his empty cup down.

"Not exactly," he said, "but I'll take that endless body of water anyway. Can't wait to crash into it and swim for days."

A mob of people let out a cry and drew my attention instantly to the bar. Flashes of Grady's obnoxiously flowered shirt were obvious through a gathering crowd. In the sea of faces, I thought I recognized Helene's parents as they joined the dinner. Both of them appeared to have lei's around their necks.

Bastian motioned to them with a tilt of his head. "Who's that?"

"Helene's parents."

"The Dunkins?" he asked.

Dagny stiffened when I nodded. "Yeah."

Bastian made a sound in his throat. "That guy has more money than we'll ever see in our lives."

I shrugged. "If he keeps holding parties here and Grady invites us, I'm good with that."

A low laugh rolled out of Bastian, disappearing as fast as it came. Dagny stared at the amassing crowd as it quaked with laughter. Her nostrils flared a bit in a glazed, half-terrified expression that was becoming all-too-familiar. I reached over and put a hand over hers. The contact sent a jolt through her. She blinked out of her thoughts and turned to me.

"You good?" I asked quietly.

She let out a long breath. "F-fine. S-sorry."

"No problem."

"L-l-lost in thought."

Her gaze had dropped to the tablecloth, darted back to the Dunkins, and then down to the tablecloth again. The base of her neck pulsed with a fast, thrumming heartbeat. My mind turned over the obvious evidence of distress and I kept a wary eye out. Something about the Dunkins made her nervous, but I couldn't imagine what. She seemed fine with Helene earlier, albeit a bit . . . off. Did they have history? Her acceptance of my offer came *after* I'd slipped Helene's name into the conversation.

Then again, why would Dagny know anything about a Texas oil tycoon?

Before I could dive too far into my thoughts over it, Bastian pushed his plate away. "Can I steal a shower in your place?" he asked. "I already told Grady not to save me a room. Brought the hammock."

Dagny shot to her feet. "Y-yes. You can use m-mine. Ours, I m-mean. Sorry . . . I'll sh-show you the w-way."

Bastian nodded, but sent me a questioning look when Dagny bent over to pick her flip flops up out of the sand. I shrugged in reply as I came to my feet, groggy from a delicious, heavy dinner in my gut. A long day of traveling, and the sound of the ocean just outside, had lulled me into a ready-to-sleep state.

Dagny's weirdness about the Dunkins—not to mention Vikram's still unknown whereabouts—could wait until the morning. For now, I wanted to stumble into bed and dream of Dagny's gentle touch on the back of my neck.

* * *

The dinner lasted into the night.

Sometime around eleven o'clock, the bar finally shut down. Half-drunk people, ready to let loose on their island adventure, filtered away. A half-hiccup-giggle combination could be heard now and then as the guests made their way through the ring of palm trees around the beach and farther onto the island. Once the dinner sounds gave way to quiet waves, I relaxed on a lounge chair under a star-studded sky.

While satellites passed overhead, I stacked my hands behind my head and let my gaze get lost in the stars. My thoughts drifted to Dagny. Victoria. Grady. Vikram. The inevitability of change. My life in Pineville seemed rigidly structured compared to Bastian, even Vik. That idea used to terrify me. Now? It wasn't so bad. Adventures helped me keep up with my wild side, but the routine kept time moving along.

Maybe the same went for Grady.

For marriage, even. Although that thought seemed far too out there to contemplate right now. Particularly with the memory of Victoria fresh on my mind. The sound of a body shuffling through the bungalow preceded a large shadow in the doorway, complete with a computer at his side.

"Have a seat," I said.

Bastian lowered onto a chair and tipped his head back to look at the same sky. For several minutes, we remained in the silence, eyes lost on the stars.

"Different here," he murmured.

"Very."

He grunted. "Easier without the smoke."

Bastian sank farther down the chair. My eyes drifted closed so I could take in the crashing waves below.

"Find Vik yet?" he asked.

"No, but his flight came in before ours."

Bastian grunted. When several minutes passed without a word, I opened my eyes again. Too much more of this and I'd fall asleep.

"What happened with Victoria and Dagny? How were you there?"

Bastian's teeth flashed in the moonlight as he released a rare, and brief, smile. "I'm always in the right place at the right time."

"Not always," I muttered.

Bastian gave a quick review of what he heard. Victoria's chummy conversation, then quick spin of the tables to turn Dagny against me. Classic move for her. We'd only spent a week or so together, and I still recognized her manipulations when I saw them.

"Dagny held her own," I said.

"She impressed me. You going to hide behind her?" Bastian asked. He shifted back, his long legs sprawled in front of him.

"Nah. I'm going to talk to Victoria in the morning."

Now that I'd seen her, talking to Victoria didn't seem so daunting. Something in breaking the spell she held over my mind removed my uncertainty. In the light of day, Victoria was beautiful, but not in the same way as Dagny. It wasn't Victoria I couldn't stop thinking about, at any rate, and that likely meant something.

"Victoria needs a line she can't cross," he said, then quietly added, "like we all do."

Several more minutes, and a murmured conversation from hotel employees cleaning up the dinner, filled the quiet. I let the ease of the day drift in and out of my chest with each breath, feeling farther and farther from my cruiser. From flashing lights. From intensity, long nights, and tough conversations.

I turned and shot Bastian a questioning glance. "You still liking wildland fire?"

He scoffed. "No, I hate it."

"You always hate it in the summer. Then you love it in the winter."

"When I'm not doing it."

I grinned. "Exactly."

He shook his head, then rubbed a hand along his tricep and shoulder. Mid-summer meant his large body had started to waste away except for a few muscle groups needed when swinging an axe and a shovel. He'd bulk back out through the winter, just in time to qualify for the Hot Shot team again, then lose it in another self-sacrificing summer of heat. There had to be something in the painful cycle that he liked.

"How much longer?" I asked.

"One more year." He shook his head. "Giving it one more year."

"Then?"

"No idea."

Bastian had never been anchored to a single career path. He taught snowboarding in the winter, fought wildland fires all summer, and did whatever he wanted on his cheap computer in the in-between. In the meantime, he stored away money like a squirrel. Until he figured out exactly what he wanted to do, he'd oscillate between the two and not say much in the meantime. He'd been like that in high school, too. A perpetual coaster.

"College?" I asked.

He shrugged. "Maybe."

Another span of silence. Bastian would be a good college student. "Vik's upset about Grady getting married," I said.

"What doesn't Vik get upset about?"

I laughed. Fair point.

"What about you?" I asked. "Grady's the first to go."

Bastian fell quiet for a moment, so I let it ride. Several long minutes later, he replied, "Good for Grady. Not the choice I'd make, but I see why he's doing it. You?"

Anytime before now, I would have said, *Same,* but this time the word stuck in my throat. Would I make the same decision as Grady? Any other time, I'd say no. It's why I avoided *abuela,* because I knew that I didn't want what she wanted.

These days, I didn't know.

"I think he might be the smartest one of all of us," I muttered, and Bastian tilted his head back and laughed.

I fell asleep with the breeze in my ear, and the song of the ocean a soft chant behind it.

Chapter Eleven

DAGNY

The crash of waves on the beach woke me the next day.

My muscles let out a long, deep sigh when I stretched, a sheet pulled tight around my waist, and luxuriated in the sound of the beach outside. Sunlight streamed through the French doors that led onto the balcony attached to my little room, falling in lovely ribbons across my bed.

Groggy, I opened my eyes. No clocks. Phone turned off. No customers, beeping machines, or annoying drive thru requests. No texts from Mom. No one to serve, clean up after, or worry about judgment with my stutter.

Not a soul to talk to.

Not a single place to be.

With a little squeal, I turned, tucked my head into the pillow, and dropped back to sleep with a happy sigh.

* * *

The gentle clank of silverware roused me sometime later.

I blinked awake and sat up. A door separated my bedroom from the main living area in the bungalow. It was propped open less than an inch, allowing me to see a body moving out there. Hernandez, I'd guess. With the heel of my hand, I rubbed my eyes and fought off a yawn. By the time I stumbled out of my bedroom and into the main bungalow area, some of the cobwebs in my thoughts cleared.

Hernandez sat on the edge of the couch, his forearms propped on his thighs as he looked at a sheet of paper. A tray filled with waffles sat on the coffee table in front of him, along with a pile of fresh fruit, orchids in a vase, and several small crocks of butter, flavors of syrup, and what appeared to be bacon bits. He glanced up, saw me, and smiled in that lopsided way that stole my breath every time.

"Hey," I croaked.

"Happy lunch." He gestured to the tray with a tilt of his head. "Thought you might be getting hungry."

I sank to the couch. "What t-time is it?"

"Noon."

My jaw dropped. "Seriously?"

"Seriously."

"Oh, I'm s-sorry. I didn't—"

"Don't worry about it. You deserve the sleep and nothing was happening anyway."

"B-but . . . there's a b-beautiful island to enjoy and explore. Are th-there things I sh-should be doing with you r-right now?"

The paper crinkled a bit as he passed it over to me. "Yoga in half an hour, if you like that kind of thing. Here's a schedule."

With a wary eye, I regarded a list of events underneath an elegant scrollwork font. What little I knew of Helene already was exactly represented in the calm elegance of this paper. Even her wedding event list was lovely. Promising for a half-sister. Maybe our DNA would give me some of those vibes one day.

My eyebrow lifted at Hernandez. "You do yoga?"

He laughed. "No, that's more Vik's thing if he's sober. But you can go if you want. Helene leads it. She's a yoga instructor or something. The rehearsal is tonight, then another dinner. But tonight is more formal. It's in an indoor atrium with a waterfall, or something." He shrugged. "The day is yours to do whatever you want."

The sleep felt amazing, that much I couldn't deny. But I didn't want to rest on the island escape or be away from Jayson. I'd never touched the ocean before, and frankly never thought I'd be able to. Pineville residents had a way of hunkering into a square radius of fifty miles and never really leaving. For some reason, I'd fallen into that. With this exotic escape around me, I couldn't fathom why.

The list of things I wanted to do today populated in my head, starting with *Kiss the breath out of Hernandez* and sliding right into *swim in the ocean naked.*

Neither of which I'd voice out loud.

At least . . . not yet.

The groove in his forehead came out next. "You mentioned needing to do something while you're here. Is that still on the table? Anything I can help with?"

The sincerity in his tone told me it wasn't a poor attempt to figure out my secret, but an actual desire to help me out. Just thinking about Anthony Dunkin sent a cold feeling into my stomach, and I had no idea what to tell Hernandez. The way I *thought* things would happen was so different from the ways they actually laid out.

Short answer: I had a lot less courage than I'd expected.

Last night, I could barely bring myself to look in Anthony's direction when I heard he had appeared. I'd glanced, but not *really* looked. My gaze had been vague, like I desperately wanted to see him, but couldn't bear to at the same time. Instead, I'd seen obscured bodies and shapes in the darkness, my stomach tied into knots that only sleep had undone.

In the light of day, it seemed so cowardly. Anthony wouldn't have known if I just *saw* him, but even a glimpse of the man felt intimate. Close. Like suddenly everything would become a little too real when the moment actually happened.

So, no. I had no idea when I'd *do that thing* I'd told him about. The NDA lay in my backpack, curled up there like a promise I still had to fulfill. But where would I corner Anthony? How would I even present something like that without destroying his life or revealing it to someone?

Once again, the dream wasn't quite the same as reality.

"Th-that," I drawled and leaned back. "I . . . I'm n-n-not entirely s-sure."

He nodded. "Well, let me know if I can help."

"Th-thank you."

We sat so close that, for a moment, I thought he'd reach over and put a hand on my knee. Our proximity was close enough that it would be so easy for him to do it, but there was no reason to pretend here. At least, not for him.

Last night's dinner with Hernandez had been easy because I finally *wasn't* pretending. For the first time since my freshman year of high school, I was allowed to let my life roll out the way that I wanted it to. With Jayson's attention riveted on me. My fingertips on top of his skin. His voice mixing with mine in quiet conversation. The bold assumption I'd had last night that he'd still want to pretend to be a couple was so unlike the normal Dagny: the scared Dagny that strove to be invisible.

But I was *tired* of that Dagny.

Maybe it was the open ocean air, the freedom of not holding back around Hernandez, or just the inevitability of change, but I sensed something stirring within me. Something new, big, and wildly bold.

Or maybe it was Hernandez.

His voice cut through my haze of thoughts. "I meant to thank you for last night."

"Th-thank me?"

"Bastian told me what happened with Victoria. What he heard of it, anyway. I'm sorry she pounced on you like that."

Victoria came rushing back to me all too soon. In the light of day, I wanted to giggle over it. What a dramatic woman. "Ah." I smiled to reassure him. "She d-didn't f-frighten me."

"I plan to talk to her today and tell her to back off."

"D-do it for your s-sake. Not mine."

He nodded. "Of course. But I still don't want her bothering you. Or me, for that matter. And . . . thank you for believing me." He frowned. "If you do, of course. Maybe Victoria has convinced you that I'm a terrible person."

My lips pressed together in a poor effort to keep from smiling. He relaxed a little when he saw it. "She was n-not successful, I p-promise. You're right, though. Sh-she's good at what she d-does."

"I wish her well, but I just want her to leave me alone," he said simply, and it tugged at my heart. What a perfect thing to say.

A strand of hair fell into my eyes as a little breeze rustled in from outside, and blushed when I realized he was staring at me. I didn't have a bra, makeup, or even a decent hair style in place. Jayson didn't seem to have noticed, and if he didn't care, I didn't either. Finally, he seemed to come back into himself and gazed away with an adorable, embarrassed little smile, like a kid.

Part of me wanted to guide his arm back onto my shoulders, then force him to snuggle with me while the breeze lulled me into yet another warm sleep, but I held back. This wasn't real behind closed doors, and that reminder might be the only thing that created a natural distance. That allowed me to walk away from this experience without my heart being a total wreck on the ground behind me.

No, I needed some space if I was going to mentally prepare for the rehearsal and rehearsal dinner tonight, where he'd inevitably have some sort of role. Traditional anything wasn't really my forte, or something I was used to. Mom didn't abide by any sort of rule book that she didn't write, so the whole wedding thing was a new world.

"I think I'll try that yoga class out." I tugged a grape off the stem and popped it in my mouth. "Where is it?"

"Out on the beach." He tilted his head in the direction the dinner had been. "Mats provided."

I gave him a little smile, then straightened up. To stop me from throwing myself into his arms, I returned to my room and shut the door firmly behind me. Then I let out a long breath, pressed my forehead into the smooth wood of the door, and tried to talk myself out of intense infatuation. The one I was supposed to be demystifying right now.

Even though there would be no returning from that torrential landslide.

The yoga class had almost started by the time I padded my way through the foliage and onto a stretch of beach where ten or eleven people were gathered. The empty beach was so wide that I could step into position at the back and never be noticed, all while creating distance between me and Jayson.

Win, win.

Vikram lingered in the milling crowd, but I acted as if I didn't see him. I didn't know him well. Of the Merry Idiots, my crush extended only to Jayson for my high school career. He left after my freshman year, but still haunted the general Pineville area until he settled into work as a deputy around twenty-one. Around then, I started to work at the Diner, and he'd come in often.

Vikram had been enigmatic and funny to a fault. Charming, in some ways. He seemed to do everything with high intensity, as if he had no medium scale. He'd sort of frightened me, and when he left the high school, it had been a bit of a relief.

Today, Vikram wore a form-fitting t-shirt across lean shoulders and a pair of board shorts. He wore his hair longer and pulled away from his face, still slightly tousled. Like Jayson, I didn't expect Vik to remember me, and I saw no flicker of recognition in his eyes when he glanced my way as I arrived. His gaze skated away, and I let out a long breath.

All the better.

Helene stood at the head of the group and sent me a subtle little wave in between conversations with Victoria and a young girl. I returned it with a warm smile and a silent pang of regret that we would never be *sisters*. A tower of yoga mats waited off to the side in the sand, and I quietly plucked one off the top and unrolled it. It had been a year or two since I'd last attempted to even stretch, so this would be interesting.

The hiss of a mat opening to my right side drew my gaze up. Bastian tossed his flip flops into the sand next to him. Before I could say another word, the same thing happened on my left. Vikram moved over there. He sent a quick nod to Bastian over my back, then winked at me.

Well . . . maybe he did remember me. Then again, Vik winked at any available female, and he knew Hernandez and I *weren't* really dating.

"Wh-what are you d-doing?" I asked Bastian, because he seemed the safer bet. He looked at Victoria, then back to me.

"Making sure she doesn't get weird again."

Vik whistled low. "Girl be crazy."

"I-I'm fine. R-really."

"Hernandez insisted." Bastian shrugged. "We obey."

That moment, Victoria turned around to face our direction, but she didn't look our way. Her hair glided over her shoulders in a ponytail that swept her bikini top. Just as Helene called for class to begin, Victoria stepped away. Unable to help myself, my gaze followed her as she strolled off the beach without looking back. Had she left because I was there? I doubted it, so I ignored her as she disappeared and tried not to think too hard about Jayson asking them to stand at my side.

Helene guided the class into a few gentle stretches that soon consumed my attention. The gentle tug and pull on my body felt refreshing after the plane ride and long, deep sleep. The breeze stirred my hair, and the sand felt hot beneath the mat. I luxuriated in the open air. How un-tropical would the coffee shop feel after this? I'd never want to go back to Mom's claustrophobic towers and wild ideas.

Only a few men freckled the female-dominated crowd, among them a middle-aged woman that looked like a wiser version of Helene. Alison Dunkin, I would bet. Helene's mother and Anthony's wife of over twenty years. I tried not to stare at her—or Vikram, who was surprisingly agile and talented for a man that drove trains for a living—while the class progressed. Bastian moved like a stiff tower, and groaned, red-faced, with every other stretch.

For years, a deep curiosity about Anthony had haunted me. Alison lingered in a close second. Questions about them had always plagued me. What was their marriage like? Were they happy? Was he a good husband? Was she a good wife?

Who got to define *good* in those roles, anyway?

Alison had captured my curiosity more than I expected because I couldn't help but wonder what she'd do if I ever popped into her awareness. Perhaps she knew about me already. Alison may have been the one that had the idea for the NDA and consideration of $50,000 to my mom.

But why stay with a husband that would do such a thing? Power, I'd guess. Money, for another. Although both might be the same thing.

These thoughts accompanied me through the deep breathing exercises, flanked by Bastian and Vikram. Still, having them at my side was bolstering. Crowds didn't seem so daunting when I had someone to talk to, and neither had asked about my stutter.

Before I knew it, Helene closed the class with a bow from her waist and a wish for good health. Bastian lay on the mat, hands stacked behind him, and tilted his face back to the sun. Vik untwisted himself from his pretzel-like position and dusted the sand off his shorts after he stood up.

I stared at Alison and wondered.

"So," Bastian drawled, "Hernandez said something about going to the grill after this. You ready?"

"D-do you always m-make plans for girls you d-don't really know?" I asked, my gaze still locked on Alison. With a sigh, I forced myself to look away. There would be no answers to my questions about her, and that left me with a melancholy feeling. Because Alison seemed like the right kind of woman with the wrong kind of man. In the meantime, I tucked the question of *what will happen to Alison when I talk to Anthony?* out of the back of my mind.

Bastian tilted his head in my direction and seemed to consider my question.

"Fair," he said. "Dagny, want to hit the grill and meet up with the man you so deeply care for?"

His choice of words hit me like a bag of bricks in the chest and scattered my senses like sand on tile. *The man you so deeply care for.* Not a hint of sarcasm, but I could tell he searched for something.

Was I that transparent?

How did he know?

"Yes." I cleared my throat when I realized my silence extended to an awkward length. Vik stared at me, eyebrows high. "I'm s-s-starving."

"Me too," he murmured, his attention focused over my shoulder. "Please excuse me."

Vik had already rolled his mat up and slung it over his shoulder. He stood with one hip cocked, his wavy, black hair shining in the light as he called to a girl in a white tank top. I grabbed my mat and turned to follow Bastian when I collided into something else. An *oomph* followed a second before I stepped back and saw only flailing arms.

"S-s-sorry!" I cried. "I d-d-didn't s-see you there. I—"

Words failed me when Alison Dunkin righted herself and glanced up, a bright smile on her face. She waved a hand through the air.

"Don't worry about it," she said, laughing. "I'm such a klutz after yoga. It's like I stretch all my brains into my muscles when I relax and breathe deeply, then I'm all over the place for the rest of the day. What's that last pose? Shava-something? I almost always fall asleep."

She'd set a hand on my arm to stabilize herself—and me, I would imagine—after our crash. The mat that she'd tucked under her arm had fallen, so I bent to retrieve it.

"H-here."

"Oh, thank you."

She beamed, then pushed her sunglasses off her face and into her hair. Her eyes were piercing and kind, a blue so dark they could have been violet. Helene had clearly inherited her graceful looks from her mother.

"And what was your name?" she asked. "You must be here with the groom."

My tongue seemed to have gotten too big for my throat. I attempted to reply, but it choked off at first. She blinked, but her smile didn't falter and she waited with an easy patience that almost made it worse.

"D-d-d-dagny," I finally managed. The word came out hard, as if my frustration could shove it out by sheer willpower. "I-I'm here with J-j-jayson Hern-nandez."

Her expression brightened. "Yes! I remember meeting him a while ago. So handsome, if you ask me."

Somehow, my brain managed to make my face smile a little. While she patted my arm and prattled about the trees and the yoga class and how she'd love to live in a paradise like this forever, my brain could only compute one single thought:

I am the child of your husband's indiscretion.

Would it destroy her world if she knew? Maybe. Alison had a bright, shining kindness about her that probably stemmed from an inherent trust. What a gift, such an idealistic view on the world.

Could I crush that?

No. That wasn't even on the table. But wouldn't it be the result? Not necessarily. If Anthony had kept me hidden this long, why not a few more years? Technically, I wasn't even supposed to know about the NDA. There could be legal ramifications on Mom for me even seeing it. If I were to break the news, the recriminations could be horrendous. And pointless. To what end would I want to destroy Alison's life?

Was the truth worth it?

"I ap-p-pologize ag-g-gain," I said with a little smile.

"The pleasure and probably the fault was mine." Her hands were warm and a little gritty with sand when she squeezed my arm. "Thank you for coming to the wedding, and you let me know when that Jayson is all dressed up." She winked at me. "Can't wait to see him in a tuxedo. Forgive me, but I best be going. Better get my sleepy husband up. He'd sleep through a hurricane with open windows."

As quickly as she came, Alison left. Someone called to her from across the crowd. She gave a little wave, and headed that direction. While going, several other women flanked her and they moved in a group as they walked away, laughing over something Alison said. Her departure felt like clouds skidding over the sunshine. Everything fell into a small darkness.

Vik had nearly disappeared down the beach, captivated by the girl, while Bastian stood several feet away, half-turned, as if he'd started to go to the grill and then realized I wasn't back there.

"You good?" he called.

"F-fine."

"I'm going to find Hernandez."

The beach had emptied while I'd stuttered my way through the talk with Alison, and I still felt as if my heart hadn't recovered from the shock. I pointed the other direction. "I'm going to sit on the beach for a minute."

After one last, studious look, he nodded and moved away.

Chapter Twelve

JAYSON

Although I hadn't seen Victoria in almost three months, I had a feeling she'd find me. Like she was a stalking cheetah. I, like a lowly gazelle, could sense that she lurked in the shadows. I didn't know where she hid, but I knew she'd be there, because there was no fighting inevitability.

And find me, she did.

Fifteen minutes after Dagny wandered to the yoga class and Bastian ditched his computer to not-so-subtly accompany her just in case, a knock came on the open bungalow door. Victoria's shadow preceded her into the room, but she stopped short of letting herself inside. I'd recognize that long, hourglass figure anywhere.

"You want to talk?" I called without looking back while I filled up an empty water bottle at the sink.

"I think I deserve it," she said. Her voice was as silky as ever. It felt uncomfortably like crinkle paper under my skin. I hid a scoff. *She* deserved it? Well, that grabbed my curiosity. With a nod, I motioned outside.

"Then we can go out on the patio."

She scoffed, her bare feet almost silent on the wooden floor. "You don't want to be alone with me?"

I laughed. "No."

Before she got within arms distance, I stepped outside and sat on a chair in view of the yoga class, water bottle in hand. Now that Victoria was here, I wanted a beer. But lowering my defenses with her around wasn't in the game plan. Maybe this paranoia was overkill for a woman that told me I'd never be good enough for her.

But, maybe not.

On the beach below, Dagny followed Helene through a stretching routine that would have made my mouth water had I been a lesser man. On purpose, I gazed away. There'd be no focusing on Victoria while Dagny moved her body like *that*.

My eyes sneaked back, though.

Three times.

Victoria settled lightly on the chair between me and the yoga party. She rolled her lips together and brushed her hair out of her face, but kept her gaze on the ocean. One leg, hidden beneath a gauzy skirt, crossed the other one. Her legs were golden perfection and happened to move a little closer to me with every moment that passed. That was fine. I wasn't a leg man.

"So." She let out a breath. "How have you been?"

"Good, and you?"

"Fine."

Our blasé tone carried into the silence. Victoria played with an errant string on her lap. "I was happy that you came," she finally said, and her voice had lowered.

"I'm glad I could make it."

"Were you?"

Her head tilted to the side a little, and I finally met her gaze. Several seconds passed before I could answer the question, and not because it startled me, but because I'd just realized that Vik stood next to Dagny down on the beach. He and I hadn't had a

chance to talk yet, and if I saw him put any advances on Dagny . .
.

With effort, I closed those thoughts and blinked out of
them.

"I was glad to make it," I finally said once I remembered her
question. "Grady and Helene are a great couple. It's an island
resort that's all-inclusive and I only had to pay for my plane
ticket and Dagny's. The math is pretty simple."

Victoria made a noise in her throat. "I thought my presence
would deter you."

"Not even a little."

She flicked a lock of hair over her shoulder. "I suppose we
should just get rid of the elephant in the room." She leaned back,
her eyes dropping. Perhaps it wasn't fair of me to turn the weight
of my most intense stare on her, but I didn't trust Victoria to
represent herself honestly. Victoria wasn't afraid of much,
certainly not a man. So when I looked directly at her with my
flattest expression, she only faltered a little.

"If there's an elephant for you," I said, "we can clear the air,
but I'm fine over here. You made your position clear, and I've
respected it."

Her nostrils flared, then relaxed. "That's . . . fair."

I blinked. She shrugged.

"That's fair," she repeated. "I can't control the way you feel."

Startled, I just waited for what would come next because
fairness hadn't been a factor before. With Victoria, there was
always a next.

"I just . . ."

She trailed off, then leaned forward and picked her words
back up. Her shoulder shifted, allowing a greater view to her
bikini top, which I ignored.

"I suppose I want closure, that's all. What we had was
special. Yes, it was fast but . . ." Her expression softened. "It was
also magical. Do you deny that?"

"*What* was magical?"

She straightened, her eyes bright. "The chemistry between you and me. We're cut from the same cloth, Jayson. We excel in whatever we do. We care about others. We aren't afraid to go against culture. I sensed that in you right away." Her hand rose to press against her heart. "Here. Even *you* said that. When we met, it was like we were meant to be."

Warning bells clanged in my head. Victoria had done this before—assigned words that had definitely never crossed my lips. Put too much meaning to normal things, making it impossible for me to escape.

Also, *she* had said we were never meant to be.

"I said what?"

"That you felt something magical for me."

I scoffed. "Sorry, I don't use that word."

She shrugged. "Special, then. The sentiment is the same."

"Is it?"

Her expression hardened. "You're going to deny it?"

"I felt you were attractive and interesting, and I was all in from the beginning. You are the one that backed away." I shrugged. "You chose, Vic."

She huffed and folded her long arms across her chest. "*That* is a lie. You were mad about me, Jayson, and I was mad about you. I don't need to make that up."

"It's true."

Her head jerked up to mine.

"But you also let me go," I continued. "And now it's too late."

She frowned. Her lips pressed back together for a moment before she shook her head. The rising tension in her cooled a bit.

"Well," she murmured, "maybe I realized my mistake."

"If that's the case, I'm sad for you. I have Dagny now and she's the real deal."

The words came out of my mouth before I knew they

existed. Hearing them startled me for only a second, because they were right. Dagny *was* the real deal. Dagny was in my court now. In fact, she'd edged Victoria so far out I couldn't even see Victoria anymore. Looking at her pouty lips now, I wondered how I ever did see anything in her.

This woman would never stand before my *abuela.*

"What are you doing with that woman, Jayson? It can't be real." She waved an airy hand toward the yoga class. "D-d-dagny."

At first, I was too incredulous to speak, but the words came out with astonishment after several long moments.

"Did you just make fun of her speech impediment?"

Heat welled up in my chest, but I forced it back. Victoria hesitated, and the flicker of uncertainty told me she realized her mistake with such an immature tactic. But did I see a true apology? No. Not a hint of actual regret.

"I'm sorry." She turned away, her voice a stone. "That was wrong and petty and low, you're right. Dagny seemed . . . fine. I'm just . . . I'm jealous of her. She has what I've wanted for months now." She glanced up. "I've missed you, Jayson."

When she said nothing further, I leaned back in the chair. It had been Vikram's advice not to ever be in a room alone with Victoria—based on all his experience with women—and now I understood why. She was trying every tactic available, and I'd almost fallen for it. Because for a moment, I almost reached out to touch her shoulder and comfort her. Some valiant part of my inner idiot couldn't help himself. Victoria looked small and frustrated and I never wanted that for her.

But I kept my hands to myself because I didn't want Victoria anymore.

"I'm sorry that you feel this way, Victoria, but there's no going back. There's nothing that will happen between us, and I hope you can accept that and move on. You deserve someone that will make you happy."

For a full fifteen seconds, she didn't say a word. Her jaw tightened several times, as if she were about to speak, but she stopped herself. Finally, her throat bobbed a little as she swallowed, then nodded.

"Fine."

She stood up and headed for the door. I stood, but remained outside by the railing. Below, the yoga session started to break apart. Dagny spoke with Alison, Helene's mother. Relief that Victoria was leaving, and with so little struggle, left me a little weak. Until this confrontation showed its ending, I hadn't realized how stressed out I'd become.

Victoria stopped before she left. She gazed over her shoulder.

"I'm sorry, too."

With that, she disappeared.

* * *

Fifteen minutes later, a knock came on my door. Vikram let himself into the bungalow, then dropped onto my couch with both arms in the air in a sign of victory. He fist pumped one of them.

"I still got it!"

He held up his phone, which displayed a new phone number across the top in bright green letters. I threw a pillow at him, then a beer. He deflected the first and caught the second with an arrogant smirk.

"Another number?" I asked.

"You know it. This lady, however, is just coming off a break up and needs a little reminder that men aren't dirtbags."

"You are."

He rolled his eyes. "I'm not a dirtbag, I'm just not a committer. There's a huge difference. You can still be good to women and not marry them. Grady's on his way over, by the way. Something about best man responsibilities or that garbage." Vik cracked the top off of his beer. "Nothing us lowly normals would know about."

Bastian entered through the back door before I could make a sarcastic quip back. Before I could toss him a beer, he grabbed his computer, opened it up, and slid back to sit on the counter. "Dagny's going on a walk," he said. "I have no idea where Victoria is. The grill is packed or else I'd recommend we go there."

I waved that off. "Don't worry about it. I'll order lunch. Hey, I talked to Victoria while you were out there."

Bastian's eyebrows rose in silent question. Vik paused, bottle halfway to his mouth. They both stared at me, eyes wide.

"Victoria came here?" Vik asked.

Bastian eyed me. "And she didn't claw your eyes out?"

"Yeah. It was fine. I just explained that I wasn't interested and was sorry that her feelings weren't returned. It's over. Communication for the win."

Vik snorted and leaned back. "She's not going to let it go."

"She will."

"She won't." Vik held up a hand. "Girls like that don't get thwarted, my friend. They aren't a second choice, certainly not to someone as normal as Dagny. Not without having the last word, anyway. Note my correctness in a week when you're full of regret for letting your guard down."

"Dagny isn't normal," I snapped. "Not the way you said it, anyway."

"She's normal, and that's not an insult. I'm just saying that you shouldn't let your guard down *just* yet."

I rolled my eyes. No, I wasn't getting into a dramatic breakup story here. Victoria, while she wasn't exactly an adult, was no problem to me or to Dagny. Her nasty remark about Dagny's stutter replayed through my mind. While I doubted Victoria would act on an impulse in a violent way . . . maybe

Dagny didn't need to be left alone in social circles, just in case Victoria got mean.

"Fine," I said. "Fine. I'll keep an eye out."

"We will too," Bastian countered. "We got her back."

Vik held up his beer in agreement.

A large, familiar body blocked the light from outside as Bastian held out a hand for a beer. I tossed it, but Grady advanced into the room and snatched it without breaking stride. He smirked at Bastian, then sat on a wicker chair across from Vik.

"Gentlemen," Grady drawled.

"Grady," we intoned together.

The bottle let out a little hiss when he popped it open, then he mirrored it with a sigh. After a long, long drink, Grady set the bottle down, leaned back and muttered, "Weddings suck."

"It's the planning that sucks," Vik cried and threw a pillow at him. "The rest of it is awesome. People. Great food. Celebrations. This is a dream! Besides, we're on a private island, you idiot. Weddings rock."

Grady glared at him. "Just don't tell anyone I'm here for two minutes. Two minutes where no one can talk to me."

"Helene hounding you?" I asked.

"Nah, it's my parents." Grady rubbed a hand over his eyes. "Mom wants me to try on my tux again, my aunt has questions about the ceremony and where she'll be standing even though we told her she'd be sitting, and my dad is complaining about the heat because he hates sunscreen." Grady threw his hands up. "I don't care about your sunscreen, Dad!"

Vikram asked Grady about the woman on the beach and her thwarted lover while I turned to Bastian. He sat with his back against the fridge, a brooding stare on his face. He glowered at his computer, then slammed it shut and set it aside. All through high school, he'd always sat on the counters.

"You good?" I asked.

He shrugged it off. I peered outside to see if I could find Dagny on the beach. She stood alone near the edge of the surf, arms at her side as she faced the ocean. What was she thinking about?

"So," Grady drawled and interrupted my thoughts. "I hear Hernandez is dating Dagny after all. You're the most on-again, off-again fake couple I've ever met."

A note of mischief in that tone didn't reassure me at all. I shot him a glare.

"Shut up."

"What?" Grady spread his hands. "You said you weren't dating on the phone, but last night she said you are. The way she looked at you over dinner . . . Let's just say that I saw her feed you that pineapple."

Oh, I would always remember that pineapple. Vik tried to hide a laugh behind a cough, but Grady didn't even attempt to hide his hoot-like laughter that always reminded me of a high-pitched owl.

"Shut up, Grady."

"He protests too much," Vik cried.

"We're not dating," I snapped, and even I heard the defensiveness in the words. "She just said that for Victoria's sake. Victoria pulled her aside and talked to her about me, so Dagny wanted to get her off my back."

Grady whistled. "Cat fight, my dude."

"No cat fights. I just spoke with Victoria. She's going to back off and get over me. Which is clearly hard to do because I'm such a stud muffin."

Vik rolled his eyes so hard he almost fell off the chair. Bastian snorted.

"Not that easy," Vik sang. "You hurt her pride, that's all I'm saying."

The uncomfortable truth was that Vik had it right. While I wanted to assume Victoria would back off, she hadn't exactly *said* as much. Most of this was wishful thinking, at best. But we were at a wedding and on an island with extremely influential people. If there was one thing Victoria would not want to risk, it was her reputation.

Or so I hoped.

"So," Vik said to Grady. "You're tying the friggin' knot."

Grady looked up and met Vik's challenging stare. Vik always kept things light, but there was an undercurrent of disbelief in his tone he didn't bother to hide. Grady held his gaze for a second and said, "Yeah."

Vik hid his response behind a sip of beer. Bastian watched both of them carefully. In all our years together, there had only ever been a few fist fights between us, and those had mostly cleared the air. Grady and Vik went at it the most. They lived on opposite sides of most opinions all their life. Grady was a classic, Vik a progressive. After a few swings, they'd not talk for a week, then we'd come back together like nothing happened at all.

I found myself hoping they'd just get the beating over with already.

"You got a problem with it, Vik?" Grady asked.

"Yes!" Vik threw his hands in the air. "Finally! Can we talk about this? Why the hell are you getting married?"

Grady motioned in front of him. "Bring it out. What's your problem with Helene?"

"Nothing. Helene is lovely."

"So why are you acting like I kicked your dog?" Grady snapped. "I'm getting married, Vik. I'm not sacrificing myself to a pagan ritual."

"Disagree," Bastian muttered, but acted like he hadn't said anything when Grady shot him a glare. Vik schooled a bark of amusement, but only barely.

When I glared at Bastian in question, he shrugged and mouthed, "Antiquated."

"You're the first to go," Vik said to Grady. He leaned

forward, his forearms leaning on his thighs. "You're breaking up what we have as brothers."

"We meet once a year to do something stupid and dangerous."

"Don't diminish all the years before it," Vik cried. "You know it's more than that, and if you're going to make it small so you can stab us in the back, that's a low blow."

"This decision has nothing to do with you."

"Exactly!"

"You want me to keep you involved in my life?"

"That would be great."

Grady blinked. "Don't be stupid, Peter Pan. We can't be idiotic teenagers forever. At some point, we have to grow up."

Vik pointed to himself. "I'm a fully functioning adult with a job and a rent payment and plenty of women that love me. I can still have fun as an adult. Don't put that adult crap argument to me, Grady. It will lose every time."

"Counter," Bastian muttered. "Fully functioning is up for debate."

Vik glared at him.

Bastian sent him an innocent look of question.

"You don't have to be married to have fun and be free," Vik said. "That's all I'm saying. You're killing our plan to be bachelors and have fun the rest of our lives."

"That was your dream, Vik," Grady said. "Not mine."

"It was ours!"

Vik shot to his feet and Grady followed. Grady was broader through the shoulders, with big hands that could span a basketball and a fierce expression that helped him navigate the most challenging situations. Vik was strong, but a scrapper. He won through sheer mental brawn and the power of surprise. In a fight, no one saw Vik's next move coming, but no one could endure Grady's raw strength.

Bastian slid off the counter to interfere, but I held him back with a shake of my head. "They need it," I muttered.

"I'm not making it small," Grady barked to Vik. "We had awesome years together, and we'll have more. But I don't have to be single and angry at women to have fun with you."

"I'm not angry at women."

"Disagree," Bastian called.

Vik flipped him the bird, then turned back to Grady.

"You can't go back, Grady. Once this ball starts rolling, it takes you down the other side of the mountain. You leave behind adventure and excitement for diapers and fences and mortgages. You know you won't make the time to do the crazy things. Not when you have a five-year-old tugging on your pant legs, or something."

"Maybe our definition of adventure differs."

Vik huffed a breath. "Fine. You're gone, I can see that. And Helene is fantastic, so I wish you the best. But you at least need to acknowledge what you're doing here. You're the trigger that changes everything we've had the last ten years. We deserve that."

"You want an apology?"

"No. I want you to *say* it."

Grady's nostril flared, and tension built in the room like a brewing storm. On some level, it felt good. Vik vented what Bastian and I had also thought, but didn't have the balls to say to Grady's face. Vik had always been the voice—mostly of insanity—but sometimes of truth. If nothing else, Vik gave everything at face value.

A shout from outside, and the sound of Grady's phone chiming against his thigh, broke the tension in the air. Grady hesitated.

"That's *your* opinion, Vik." He moved forward to clap a hand on Vik's shoulders. "I'm always glad to have it. My opinion is different, because I want the fence, the diapers, the five-year-old, and the woman in my arms every night. I respect your decision not to have it, and want you to respect mine. Got it?"

Vik nodded once, his expression flat. "Got it."

Grady straightened. "Now, my wife is texting me, and I need to go." He looked at me then. "Best man, you want to say anything at dinner tonight?"

"Do you need me to?"

He lifted an inquiring eyebrow. "No, but you're going to have a speech for the actual reception dinner, right?"

"It's going to make you cry, my friend."

Grady tried to shove me into the fridge as he passed in an attempt to force levity back in the room. "The only thing that'll make me cry is how bad the three of you smell. I'm out. See you tonight."

Chapter Thirteen

DAGNY

Warm sand crept between my toes, all at once solid and crumbly.

After running into Alison at the yoga class, my bones felt like liquid. The motivation to hold Anthony accountable that had bore me up all these years suddenly floated away. Meeting Anthony and waving the NDA in his face was one thing.

But his wife?

Although I had only known her for a few minutes, her warmth and brightness sent my mind careening on a different path that I'd never considered before. The path of subtlety around my biological father. Quiet. All my life I'd wanted to live under the radar except for this one thing: confronting Anthony Dunkin.

Now, all I could think about was the other side of things. The side that Alison illuminated with her innocent smile and warm acceptance. And what about gentle Helene? I hadn't expected to like her so much. Their comfortable life was built on a gossamer web of lies. Was Mom one of many other women? Had Anthony done this before? Maybe there were several NDA's floating out there.

What if the one-night stand with Mom was just an accident?

Did cheating get to be an accident? They'd likely been drunk at the time—Mom once swore that the last time she ever let alcohol cross her lips was when I was conceived—but did that make them less responsible for the outcome?

No.

Except Alison wasn't "responsible" for my existence either. Yet, she'd have, or even already had, a burden to bear in the scenario. Perhaps that was just life. The cumulative result of choices made out of our control, but that still affected us. Sometimes drastically.

All this time I'd been motivated by a self-righteous indignation against the decision Anthony made *for* me. He decided for me that I wouldn't get him as a father, and his absent legacy and cold reception to the pregnancy led to a natural wariness of men for my mother.

Why did *I* get set aside?

Why wasn't I worth the truth?

But now I couldn't help but wonder if Anthony had so much to lose, he just couldn't bring himself to do it. Not over a child that would only make everything fall apart. Didn't the Dunkin name have generations of wealth behind them? With that kind of family came expectations and pressure, which could have all crashed because of a rash decision made while drunk.

No, he didn't get off the hook because of family privilege. No one forced alcohol down his throat. Perhaps his decision to let me go and sign over all parental rights hadn't felt personal to him at the time, but it had been personal to *me*.

My thoughts agitated like the water because I could, unfortunately, see both sides of the situation. As a child, it had never added up. How could a parent ignore a part of them walking in the world? Weren't children just portions of the soul embodied in different people? As an adult, I saw the shadows and shades of gray in the issue. It still didn't sit right, but maybe it didn't ache as much these days.

Amidst all of it was the ringing hollow of the question: *why?*

A storm swept closer to the sun, while the rest of the world remained a bright, endless blue behind me. Like a reminder that storms occupied or darkened some—but not all—of our space.

A voice interrupted my dark reveries.

"Hey."

I turned to find Jayson there, and the warm smile on his expression swept the angst out from under me. He sat on the sand next to me. I smiled, relieved to have someone whisk me away from such a depressing back-and-forth.

"Hey."

"How was yoga?"

He wiggled a little as he situated himself in the sand, then put his arms on his bent knees. Wind whipped by from the inward-bound storm, churning the waves into higher peaks. The first tendrils of the cloud bank slid in front of the sun and sent a shadow across the sand. The burning prickle of sunshine on my skin faded for a moment, and I enjoyed relief from the intense warmth.

"Ff-fine. It's been a w-while since I've t-tried it." I lifted an arm and rubbed the back of it, where the muscles felt more stretched than sore now. In the aftermath, it really did feel good.

"Vik swears by it," he said idly, "because men rarely attend yoga classes and women tend to love a yogi, I guess, but I could never get into it."

"Did you tell B-bastian to do it with me?"

"Not guard you, or anything. He wanted to see if he could stretch out his forearms because they fall asleep at night after all his saw work. I told him to keep an eye out for you if Victoria was around." He met my gaze. "I know you can take care of yourself. I've seen you at gunpoint and you were cool as a cucumber."

The reminder sent a little barb into my chest. I'd spent years of my life picturing Jayson rescuing me from various terrible situations, like a true hero coming to life. Of all of them, *that* was the one I'd never imagined. Now he'd always remember it and I wasn't sure if that was a good or a bad thing.

"N-not that c-cool," I said.

"I spoke with Victoria while you were at yoga." He leaned back, palms pressed into the sand. He wore a pair of board shorts and no shirt. It took all my considerable mental strength and concentration not to stare at the muscles that moved across his back with each breath, or gently pat away the grains of sand on his shoulder. Only his chosen topic took me away, and I kept a heavy gulp at bay.

Was he still in love with her?

Did he want to reunite?

Maybe I'd been hasty in my suggestion that we act like we were dating. Now maybe he wanted an out and my vacation was about to crash and—I forced my mental spiral to halt. Several moments had passed and it would be awkwardly quiet soon.

"Oh?"

"I think she'll leave us alone."

The easy way *us* rolled off his lips caught me by surprise, and my stomach smoldered with it. As if we were a unit. A pair. Meant to be instead of just pretending to be to get Victoria off his back. In those moments when it was easier to pretend, it was also easier to get lost in the dream.

Relief followed quickly. If nothing else, he didn't want to chase her. Jayson had never been much of a ladies' man through the years. He seemed too busy doing other things— most of them dangerous—that he didn't pay much attention to dating. Such an attitude had made things tolerable for me. I wasn't sure I could sit by and watch him ogle someone like Victoria.

"G-good. She d-doesn't frighten me."

Why I insisted on him knowing that, I wasn't sure, but it felt important enough to emphasize. Did I want him to see me as courageous the way I saw him? Yes. Like I still wanted to fit into the special Merry Idiots club, or something.

"I know."

There seemed to be nothing left to say, so we both fell quiet. I closed my eyes and tried to soak up the sounds, the grit of sand, the brush of wind. Then I felt a gentle, warm touch on my arm and my eyes fluttered back open. I looked up to see Jayson grinning at me, his palm on my arm, just above my elbow.

"Want to go swimming?"

I hesitated, glanced at the water, then back to him. A slight blush crept up my cheeks as I swallowed.

"I c-c-can't s-s-swim," I whispered. Mom had a thing against the reservoir water and swore that amoebas lived in it, so we never went near the lake. Pineville didn't have a swimming pool —at best a few knee-deep creeks with winter snowfall—so water hadn't ever been a big part of my life.

"Stay with me and I'll keep you safe. Deal?"

I sucked in a sharp breath, stuck on the precipice of *don't you dare get closer to him* and *take this opportunity right now!* Serafina would kill me if I didn't go with him and I could mentally hear her excited squeal when I told her. Finally, my heart won out over common sense, even though the battle was gory.

I smiled.

"Let's d-d-do it."

* * *

Ten seconds later, I seriously regretted my hasty excitement.

Jayson tugged me down the beach, a kid-like haste apparent through his whole body as we headed to the water. I wore a tank top and loose shorts over a tankini, an outfit Serafina had picked out because the turquoise color made my skin pop. But I hadn't bought any of this with the intent to *swim* in it.

Now, we plowed right toward the ocean.

"I-I-I r-really d-don't know the w-water all that w-w-well."

The surf splashed his ankles and splattered my legs. His fingers interlaced with mine, tightening his grip.

"I got you, Dagny."

The words, so simply spoken, nearly gave me a heart attack. How many years had I dreamed of those words? How many times when I was lonely, the world was dark, and my quiet heart wanted a hero, had I thought of him saying those things? He threw them out so carelessly now, as if the sentiment cost him nothing.

When, to me, it was everything.

"B-b-but—"

My protestation slowed when we slipped into the warm waves. They played around my calves and slid back, taking sand away from under my feet. The water was deliciously perfect and a silky caress on my bare skin. Humidity lay thick on the air as the sun slipped behind the storm cloud. Wind danced past me, a gentle breath on my cheeks.

Well, maybe it wouldn't be so bad in the water.

"It is n-nice," I said with a sigh.

"It's better when you're all the way in it."

So many thoughts spiraled around me. The massive ocean, ready to drown me. The way the waves tugged and pulled. Undertows. Sinking and not being able to get back to the top. But it wasn't as scary as it could have been, because he held onto my hand. He gently pulled me closer, keeping me near his overly-capable strength. Jayson was oblivious to the mental screaming in my head. He kept going into the water with a steady chatter that eased some of my tension. Hearing his voice, feeling his hand in mine? Yes, I'd head toward one of my greatest fears if he were at my side.

"See?"

The water lapped around my shoulders now. Unlike the

reservoir, which was chilly in the summer, this felt like the perfect bath. I eyed the waves, but they were mostly gentle roars as they hurried by. He still hadn't let go of my hand, which I'd locked into mine with a tight grip. I barely managed to keep from clutching him as close as possible.

"N-not bad."

He grinned. "You don't like water?"

"I d-d-do."

"You never swam in the reservoir?"

My mom has a deathly fear of amoebas and dark water, I thought, but lightly said, "N-not much."

A fastidious wave crashed over my shoulders and slopped around my neck unexpectedly. I gasped as water filled my ears. Drops dotted my lip with a salty tang. Jayson tilted his head back and laughed. Spray decorated his hair with a few sparkling glimmers, and all levity fell out of me like a bottom dropping out.

He was so beautiful.

He moved closer to me, no doubt in an attempt to help me feel safer, but it only made everything worse. My gaze darted to the empty beach and back. We weren't far from the bungalow, and far enough out that people wouldn't recognize us unless they walked into the surf. Based on the empty beach, I didn't think that would happen.

There was no reason to pretend here, but I had a feeling he *wasn't* pretending. And that was more frightening than anything else. Another wave slapped the side of my face and I gasped again.

He laughed again, but pulled me closer. Something in the pillar of his body next to mine stabilized me in the water, but it also set my heart to racing. One of his hands lingered near my waist under the water, and I felt an occasional brush from his fingertips. Chills skimmed my back everytime.

"They often come in three," he said. "So there will be—"

His words drown in another crash of ocean water into my

left ear, this one bigger than the others. Shocked by the sudden, wet slap, I sucked in a sharp breath. Water filled my nose as the wave swept me down. He tightened his hold and pulled me out of the water seconds after I dropped, but it still felt like a frightening eternity passed before I found air again.

"You good?"

Sputtering, I hold onto his forearms to regain my breath. My nostrils burned from sea water as the waves slid away until it was only waist deep again. The storm that had agitated the waves passed steadily through, but the ocean carried the rage from it now.

I tried to answer, but only coughed.

"Hold on," he called.

His arms came around me as he braced his legs and put his back to the sea. Seconds after, another wave crashed into us, but he was immobile as a rock against it. We swayed in the movement together. He pulled away, soaked, but sparkling. A wide smile covered his face, and I thought the raw touch of his skin on mine would burn marks into me.

"You good?" he asked again.

"F-fine." I nodded, even though my face and throat burned. "Th-thanks."

"You get used to the feeling of salt in your throat, I promise. C'mon, I'll show you how to body surf now that you're already soaking wet."

I stopped to peel off my tank top, then chuck it back to shore. He glanced back, then quickly away, without saying anything. I kept a wary eye on the water as we stepped back into the deeper area, closer to the waves. Maybe I could pretend like I was scared and get his arms back around me again.

"D-don't you have b-best man d-duties or something?"

He shrugged. "I'd rather be out here with you."

Part of me wanted to slap him for saying the exact right thing. For stretching my heart out to a size bigger when it was already too big for him. But the greater part of me wanted to tackle him into the water and *really* give my lungs a reason to burn. The idea of kissing the breath out of him swept me into a short fantasy that I forced myself out of.

No, I shouldn't go there.

Couldn't.

Wouldn't go there.

This vacation had an expiration date. When we returned to Pineville, would I be the same Dagny as before? Probably. Normal life and routines had a habit of sucking the fun and adventure out of life. I'd be the barista in jeans and a sloppy bun again.

And to what end?

Why did *that* have to be my future?

Ever since graduating high school, I'd made myself the promise of tracking down Anthony Dunkin. It was the only promise I'd ever made myself, even though I had other focuses, like college. The promise to find the man responsible for me, even though he'd put a price tag on my worth and turned his back without another word, had kept me going. When I hadn't battled for survival the past few years, I worked hard for that promise.

Now, I'd found him.

When I returned to Pineville, there'd be an empty loft *and* an empty purpose. Even the pallet furniture had been a means to save money to finally meet him, so what was there to save for now? Something. But I didn't know what yet. Like a buoy set adrift on tempestuous waters.

This trip was about more than helping Hernandez and my slapping eyes on my biological father. This trip closed a door when I didn't have another one to open. An ending with no new beginning.

Which made it feel a bit like a betrayal when Jayson Hernandez and his warm arms, thick shoulders, and boyish smile trapped me in sweet affection that wasn't even fake. No one watched from the beach. No one was here to impress or frighten away. What he gave to me today was sincere. The gift I had *always* wanted. And I felt like I couldn't take it, because where could we go from here? If it was right back to normal life, my heart would crush in new ways it never had before.

"You want to learn how to body surf?" he asked, and reached out for my arm when another round of waves moved past us. This time, he'd taken us out farther. The water lapped round my neck, but the waves didn't break on top of my head here. Instead, they lifted us higher and I floated in a stomach-lightening sensation that I could get used to. They broke closer to shore, so I felt safer here.

"Wh-what is b-body surfing?" I asked.

He nodded toward the waves. "Some people get small boards, smaller than surfboards, and ride these waves on their stomach. You don't need one. You can just ride these waves in toward the shore with your body."

"Sh-show me?"

"My pleasure."

He winked and shook his head, clearing the water droplets that had collected at the end of his hair, which curled slightly. A second later, I thanked my instinct to have him go first as he drifted by, muscular back flashing, and attempted to ride in on a wave that deposited him underneath a curl of white foam instead. He came up sputtering and laughing, which made me giggle.

The storm over the sun cleared as I attempted to body surf for the first time and the second. Light glimmered its way from under the clouds while I sometimes surfed successfully, but mostly tried to not die. A few people appeared here and there on the beach, but no one came into the water with us. We laughed, splashed, and he saved me more than once. His touch felt like fire against the temperate water and silky sea foam.

Finally, drenched from playing, I sat on the shoreline to catch my breath. How long had passed? Hours? Water crashed around my toes and drifted past, then slipped back by. Hernandez settled at my side, breathless from laughing.

"Thanks." His white teeth flashed for a moment with a quick smile. "It's been awhile since I've just . . . had fun."

"W-without risking your l-l-life, you m-mean?" I quipped.

He snorted and rubbed a hand through his hair to clear the water out of it. "Yeah, I guess. I mean, that's fun, but it's also something else. It's intensity more than fun. Challenge, maybe?"

I made a sound in my throat. Many had been the times that I questioned his idiocy, particularly after watching glimpses of the C-tape with Bastian and his other friends. I thought climbing into a stove-sized cardboard box with a helmet on and pushing it down the stairs was the most cringe-worthy one.

Even more times I had wondered if Hernandez just wouldn't come back to school one day because they'd taken things too far. My fragile heart with spun-sugar-strength hadn't been able to take it then, and it seemed even scarier now. Like the stakes had increased, and though he wasn't mine, there was suddenly more to lose.

Which is why my heart nearly stopped when he put a hand under my chin and quietly asked, "What are you thinking so hard about, Dagny?"

The ocean waves rolled around us, warm at my waist like a hug before it slipped away. When had we gotten so close to shore? I forced my mind back to his question. I didn't want to answer it. I couldn't have lied to him if I wanted to, and my voice slipped into the melodic timber on its own.

"I'm thinking about you."

Water dotted his thick eyelashes. His arm found my waist, hooked it, and pulled me closer. I slipped into him without resistance.

"What about me?" he asked, voice husky and low.

There was no space to answer. I didn't know who moved first, but all of a sudden his lips crashed to mine. The surf must have slammed into my back, but I felt only the pressure of his hand on my neck as he stabilized us in the waves. The slant of his lips competed with mine. The grit of sand beneath my palm as I braced myself against his gentle, loving attack. Awareness came back into me all at once when he pulled away. Only a breath apart, we stared at each other.

He looked at my lips, then back to my eyes. His chest rose and fell. My mind couldn't get around the insecure high school girl in my mind.

Jayson. Hernandez. Just. Kissed. Me.

"Was that okay?" he whispered.

I nodded.

He came back.

This time, he pushed me back until my body crashed onto the sand. Water slipped by with a gentle hiss. The kiss was hungry, his lips hot as the sun. All my resistance to what would happen when we returned to Pineville faded as I wrapped my arms around his neck and closed all space between us. His skin, slippery from the salty ocean, burned on top of mine.

Words tied up in my throat until I couldn't have spoken if I wanted to. They didn't need to be said. Jayson was like a tidal wave with power of his own. His lips kept mine, gentle as the breeze. I grabbed his shoulders to cling to him as the water rushed around us. The warmth of the sun was nothing compared to his body over me. Nothing to the heat that boiled under my fingertips on his skin. The electric feeling of his lips *finally* on mine.

The sense of this being a dream, a vivid recollection of what I'd always wanted but never believed would happen, washed through me. It swept me into the moment and I let go.

My hands threaded into his hair with all the pent-up ferocity I'd held back since high school. A subdued cry followed from somewhere deep in my chest. I kissed him harder, and he responded. I held him tighter, and he clutched me to him. The waves and the water and the ocean ceased to exist as I melted into Jayson Hernandez.

I gasped when he finally broke us apart. He leaned to the side, his forehead pressed to my shoulder, as I gathered my brain back together. Water glided past again, gentle this time. A subtle reminder of our tie to the world. My heart slammed in my chest. The sea had begun to calm, the sun to sparkle as the storm passed fully through.

"Wow," he whispered.

I held myself against him because my heart had crumbled into pieces, and his power was about to sweep them away.

Just like the tide.

Chapter Fourteen

JAYSON

We didn't speak for an hour.

After I held her in the waves while my body calmed down and my mind spun, we walked slowly back to the bungalow. Silently, she released the hand I'd forgotten she was holding and faded into her room with a hesitant smile and no eye contact. I stared out at the ocean, water pooling on the wooden floor beneath me.

My mind had broken.

Kisses were nothing new, and something I'd always taken for granted. A quick fix, maybe. A way to have the thrill, make a claim, something. They certainly weren't startling. They weren't powerful. They weren't . . . connecting.

Until Dagny.

I stood at the window, my teeth sinking into my bottom lip. Although I looked right at the sparkling ocean, I didn't see it. My mind shifted back to the salt water taste on her lips. The feeling of her hair in my hands. Her body pressed against mine.

What had I done?

All those years, Dagny lived under my nose like a shadow, never stirring anything up, never really known. We'd lived around each other, but never really spoken to one another. Now, she stood like a startling beacon of everything I could have ever wanted in my life.

And I'd wasted all that time.

* * *

An hour later, her bedroom door clicked open.

I stood up from where I sat on a wicker couch full of over-stuffed pillows. Dagny stepped out in a fluttery sundress the color of an emerald, with a diamond pattern of light green and gray. She wore her glossy hair down past her shoulders, where short sleeves barely capped the top of her arms. Her face looked bronzed from our time in the sand earlier, and my heart did a double beat at the sight of her.

Somehow, in the last hour, I imagined all that had been a dream. The kiss. The fun. The ease of being together. Her touch felt so natural in a world where I'd been trained to keep my distance. Until Dagny's hand had been in mine, I didn't realize how thirsty for physical connection I'd become. Seeing her stand before me made it clear that this was no dream.

Or it was the best dream ever.

"Hey," I said as I stood. A stupid, lopsided smile was on my face, but I couldn't have taken it off if I wanted to. Vik would have laughed at my less-than-smooth greeting to such a lovely woman. She stood just outside her bedroom, an expression of indecision on her face while she chewed on her bottom lip.

"Ab-bout earlier?"

I nodded to encourage her, but didn't dare move. Her nostrils flared. She opened her mouth, then closed it again with a perplexed expression. To my surprise, I thought I knew exactly how she felt. I wasn't even ready to go there yet.

"How about we go to the dinner," I said, "and talk about

this later? It was just a kiss, right? Doesn't have to mean anything."

Something I couldn't read flickered through her eyes, then faded. Her shoulders slumped a little, but she gave a little smile.

"Y-yes, p-please. Th-thank you."

I felt like an idiot as she fidgeted with her fingers, then tried to hide doing so. Did I take it back? Elaborate? No, that made everything worse. What had I been thinking? Only an idiot would say that.

Of course that kiss meant *something*—it meant everything—but she looked so frustrated that I wanted to spare her the agony of getting the words out. The pain of commitment when that wasn't what she wanted. For all I knew, she only wanted a vacation and couldn't have cared less about me.

Relieved for an out, I held out my arm. "Then let's get to the fondue. Thankfully, it's not my turn to make a toast yet."

Dagny put her arm through mine and we stepped out of the bungalow to head toward the hotel. The sun hung in a bright blue sky as we joined several other couples making their way across the sand and toward an atrium in the middle of the island.

"S-sand in fl-lip-fl-lops is *so* annoying," she muttered. Grains of sand skittered ahead of and behind her as she waded through.

"You can go barefoot, you know. It's an island. No one cares here."

She smirked, but it seemed half-hearted. Dagny always struck me as an introverted person, but she'd spoken more than I expected on our trip. I began to wonder if she'd been hiding all this time. A reaction to her speech impediment, or something. Tonight, after playing so much in the sun and enjoying the sound of her voice, the quiet between us seemed all-encompassing.

Even a touch tense.

A few minutes later, we stepped into the hotel atrium.

Everything sparkled, from the glasses on the table to the

silverware that looked like *actual* silver. Dagny's gaze darted from person to person with that keen curiosity she usually had, but never truly indulged through conversation. Waiters bustled around with covered trays or glasses of champagne, and the general air of money lingered in the room.

It only made me more tense.

Victoria's words when she broke things off with me whispered through my mind far too often. *There's just no stability in law enforcement, whether it's time or money. I want someone that can be with me and provide for all the things that I want and need. I don't think you can do that on your salary.*

A direct jab to a man's pride, particularly when the backdrop of her life was *this*. To her credit, she'd been right. My world would never collide with this one. For that, I was immensely grateful. No pressure to be and provide something I couldn't in a relationship, but it took coming back to this to realize it.

I held Dagny's arm a bit closer to my side.

"It's l-lovely," she said quietly.

"A bit much, if you ask me."

She smiled a little, but didn't disagree. Several long tables filled the room with their white tablecloths and elegant arrays of flowers in the middle. A sideboard across the room dripped with platters of hors d'oeuvres near which a few people mingled. Waiters swished in and out of the kitchen, bringing more food to people in the crowd.

"Wh-what would you p-prefer to this?" she asked.

"A beer at the Diner."

"N-not c-coffee at the shop?" She attempted to sound scandalized, but it came out as more of a laugh than breathy shock. I grinned.

"Black, n—"

"No c-cream or s-sugar," she said, interrupting me. Her voice dropped an octave in a poor imitation of me. "L-like a man. Five stars."

I laughed. "Okay, point taken. I have my patterns."

"Y-yes," she murmured, "you do."

A bright red, sequined dress slipped close out of the corner of my eye, and I looked over in time to see Victoria approach alone. Before this trip, I'd rarely seen her by herself. Men or other women always accompanied her. She reached out to put a hand on my arm, but I grabbed a passing wine glass and she withdrew a second before the rejection would have been blatantly obvious.

"You look as handsome as ever," Victoria said to me, as if Dagny weren't standing less than an inch from my side. Dagny's smile had become fixed, but I could have sworn I saw more intrigue than concern.

"Thank you," I said.

Victoria paused, as if waiting for more, then motioned to the table. "I've already claimed a seat at this table." She motioned to a round one not far from a table with seashell clasps holding cloth napkins together. "Would you care to sit next to me?"

I opened my mouth to protest, but another couple in deep discussion slid into place instead, oblivious to Victoria's attempts. Someone rapped a fork on a glass in a delicate tinkle that floated above the crowd.

"Attention!" called a distant voice. "Ladies and gentlemen?"

People quieted as they looked to the front of the room. The rest of the attendees funneled to tables nearby, or crossed the room to their seats. Victoria pressed her lips together, but before she could respond, Dagny motioned to two seats on the other side of the table.

"H-how ab-bout across from you?" she asked Victoria.

Victoria gave a bland smile. "Perfect."

After everyone found a seat, a quick thank you speech came from Grady's parents who ran the dinner. An army of waiters appeared from a pair of swinging doors at the back. The cleared area between tables filled with the delicious smell of food and the song of ice water filling glasses. Dagny leaned closer to me.

"D-do you know anyone here?" she asked.

I shook my head.

Her nose wrinkled. "Is th-that normal for a b-best man?"

"Probably not." I muttered. "Grady could have chosen someone more immersed in his world for this job. I'm more a remnant of his past than a daily part of his life now. But the Merry Idiots have never done anything the normal way."

Her face illuminated as she grinned and quietly said, "Touché."

Victoria's voice sailed over the clink of plates and silverware as a salad plate appeared in front of us from our right hand side. "So," she said brightly, her lips pulled into a candy-apple-red smile that matched her dress. "Tell us what you do for a living, Dagny."

The other four people at the table gazed politely at us. Dagny's face heated a little, but she responded easily.

"I'm a b-barista."

Victoria's eyebrows rose. "Oh? Like at a coffee shop?"

Dagny nodded.

"Interesting." Victoria leaned forward. "And are you doing that while you attend college?"

"Y-yes. I'm d-doing an online d-degree. The sh-shop is my f-full time j-job."

"What is your major?"

"C-construc-ction m-anagement."

Victoria's gaze became one of polite disinterest. She had a sip of water. The two women to my left—Grady's distant cousins, I thought—fell back into conversation together. An older couple with white hair and bored expression acted like they couldn't hear us.

"That's lovely," Victoria finally said, but her smile cut in a frosty way. Dagny ignored it and reached for her water. "Is Jayson a customer of your store?"

"It's n-not m-my store." Dagny had a casual sip. "I j-just work there."

Victoria's smile became more polite. I almost reached over to grab Dagny's hand in a show of solidarity, but held back. Her stare had honed in on Victoria as well, as if the two of them sensed something in the other. Whatever was about to happen here, I had no idea.

"Of course," Victoria purred. "I'm sure it's lovely having a job with so little personal responsibility. Do you live at home?"

Dagny's hand on her lap clenched. "No, I rent a studio."

"Ah."

Victoria gazed away, as if she couldn't find another topic for the two of them to discuss. I let out a mental sigh of relief. If that was—

"And what plans do you have for your future?" Victoria asked.

Dagny hesitated, and I couldn't help but feel curious myself. How had I not asked her the same question?

"I'm an o-o-open b-book," she finally managed, her voice thicker than before. Victoria smiled, and the acerbic tension seemed to catch the attention of the older guy next to her. He frowned at her.

"How very lovely for you," Victoria purred. "I imagine it's an interesting life when you can live so simply and without much progress into more important things."

Dagny's nostrils flared. "Th-that dep-p-pends on your d-definition of p-p-progress."

Victoria brightened. "Indeed. Shall we debate the point?"

"Ah . . ."

Confusion clouded Dagny's features. Victoria had set her off course a bit, and probably on purpose. Victoria waved a hand as if to dismiss the suggestion before Dagny could respond.

"No, of course not. That wouldn't be fair to you after all my extensive debate experience. Can you tell me more about how you and Jayson met? If these questions are too difficult or make you uncomfortable, do tell me to stop. I imagine it must be hard for you in social settings."

My nostrils flared and I opened my mouth to say something, but Dagny put a hand on my leg. The weight and warmth startled me out of my thoughts.

"N-not at all," she said brightly. "D-does my st-stutter bother you, Victoria?"

The direct jab back brought everyone at the table into the conversation. The two women next to me stopped pretending to be in discussion and instead looked at Dagny and Victoria. The older couple blinked back to life, mouths half open and slack.

Victoria's smile dropped into an expression of horror.

"Of course not! I'm impressed that you manage to get out at something like this and still get your point across. I do a lot of volunteer work with clinics that serve people who struggle with what you have. Very brave."

Dagny's nostrils flared, but she didn't even credit that condescending comment with a response.

"You l-lived with th-the D-dunkins, I heard?" Dagny asked. "Wh-what a l-lovely p-privilege, to b-be the r-recipient of such h-hospitality."

Victoria's fingers tightened around the stem of her wine glass. The old man coughed into his water. Eyes riveted on Victoria, his wife gave him a hard pounding on the back that only made it worse.

"They were very kind," Victoria said graciously.

"W-were you unab-ble to f-find a j-job after c-college?"

"A brief sabbatical, if you will, before I began my career."

Dagny smiled, but it had a touch of use. "H-how n-nice to live s-s-so simply and w-w-without much progress into m-more important things."

Victoria's nostrils flared. The old lady let out a squeak. Grady's cousins clear their throat, heads turned to the side and lips twitching. Only extensive training and years of law enforcement work kept me from hooting laughter. Dagny didn't even flinch—her gaze had honed in on Victoria like a pointer. The two of them stared hard at each other until I loudly broke the tense air with a comment directed to the woman at my left.

"You're Grady's cousins, right?"

She smiled. "Yes."

We fell into a polite back-and-forth until the general air of tension dissipated in the crowd. Dagny motioned for a waiter to refill her glass. Victoria gazed out, as if bored. Despite the repartee clearly meant to embarrass Dagny, she maintained a serene-like expression. Her attention turned to the older woman next to her, whom she trapped in conversation about a broach she wore. Victoria's stare flitted to me every other second, but I ignored her. Thankfully, she remained silently brooding, overlooking the crowd here and there. Grady's two cousins ignored her entirely.

Beneath the easy conversation that resumed at the table was a low-level hum of something. Frustration, perhaps. Maybe even astonishment. Then again, maybe that was just the way I felt about the situation.

Dagny laughed at something the older woman said, and the sound sent a jab through my heart. My gaze fell on Victoria, who brightened a little when she caught my stare. Her lips moved, silently saying, "My room. Later."

I gazed away in a pointed no.

She smiled a little too widely for the next hour.

* * *

By the time we broke free from the rehearsal dinner, the clock betrayed a late 10:30. Hours of smiling, talking, and monitoring a very quiet Dagny on my arm had exhausted every mental resource I had. All I wanted to do was drop into a deep sleep.

Or kiss Dagny again.

Could go either way.

When I guided Dagny out of the atrium and into the moonlit night, she gave no protest. Her eyes were drawn and tired, like she had a headache, and I wanted to get her back to the bungalow before someone else who was half drunk trapped us in conversation I didn't care about. Three hours of this was more than enough for any best man. Where Sebastian and Vik ended up, I had no idea. Somehow, I'd only caught glimpses of them all night. My friends hadn't even crossed my mind since I saw Dagny on the beach in her tankini and wanted to spend time with her. What a strange feeling.

Dagny tugged me to a stop.

"S-sorry," she mumbled. "Just a s-sec. I need to f-fix my flip flop."

She withdrew her arm from mine and bent over to fix something on her shoe. I glanced to the bungalow, glowing behind us with strings of lights and green fronds. Melodic music filtered from the atrium at our backs, a gentle form of island reggae, and the sound of laughter rolled with it.

"Oh, sh-shoot." She muttered something under her breath. "It b-broke." She straightened up, holding a flip-flop with one side popped loose.

"Do you have others?" I asked.

"Yeah, j-just back at the b-bungalow."

"We're heading there anyway."

When she straightened up, she kept an eye on her other shoe while she started forward and didn't see the couple just ahead. I opened my mouth to warn her, but couldn't speak fast enough. Dagny crashed into Anthony Dunkin with an *oomph* and started to fall backward. Before she crashed into the sand, Anthony reached out and caught her arms.

I swore under my breath as I helped her stabilize.

"Are you okay?" Anthony asked.

Dagny froze, her eyes wide, and stared at him. Her mouth dropped into a shocked *o* and she made no sound. I put a hand on her shoulder as Anthony looked her over.

"I'm sorry about that," he said. "I wasn't paying attention. Are you hurt?"

"Oh, hello!" Alison Dunkin called with a smile brightened by a few glasses of wine, I'd bet. "Dagny, was it?"

Dagny's mouth bobbed open and closed for a moment before she nodded. With effort, she looked to Alison.

"Y-yes. G-g-g-g-ood to s-s-see you."

Alison beamed at me. "And Jayson, so good to see you again." Before I could check on Dagny, Alison pulled me into a quick, warm embrace. "I'm glad you were able to make it. You mean so much to Grady."

"Thank you for inviting us," I said.

Anthony stepped away from Dagny, but kept a wary eye on her. His gaze tapered, then he shook his head as if to clear his thoughts. "Forgive me," he murmured to Dagny. "Do I know you? You seem . . . familiar."

Dagny dropped her gaze, but she looked back at him now. She shook her head, mute. Her expression had become very pale.

Something was definitely wrong.

"Good to see you again, Alison and Anthony," I said to clear the suddenly strange air. "If you'd excuse us, we need to—"

"A stutter?" Anthony asked Dagny. "Is that what I heard?"

Something fierce welled up inside of me, but before I could rescue her, her head shot up. She stared at him, wide-eyed.

"Wh-what?" she whispered.

He smiled, and not unkindly this time. "I recognize a fellow sufferer when I meet one," he said gently. "I had a stutter for years, especially as a young man. The right speech therapist worked wonders for me, although it still arises from time to time. Have you ever worked with one? If not, I'll send you mine. She's a whiz."

Dagny shook her head, more shocked than ever now. I couldn't decide if I was annoyed, impressed, or shocked by Anthony's straightforward tackling of the topic. From one sufferer to another, however, I imagined it felt more like solidarity than an imposition. Dagny looked like she was about to throw up.

Anthony held out a hand.

"Excuse me, I haven't introduced myself. I get excited when I meet another person with a speech impediment, and then neither of us can talk." He laughed, a rolling sound, and I smiled to save face. Dagny didn't even flinch, just looked at him as if she'd seen a ghost. "I'm Anthony Dunkin, father of the bride. We're grateful to have any of Grady's friends here."

"D-d-dagny," she whispered.

"Good to meet you, Dagny."

Color returned to her haunted face. She straightened her shoulders a bit and regained some of her usual presence back.

"G-good to m-meet you as well. Th-thank you f-for . . .f-for the lovely island es-scape. F-forgive me, b-but my sandal broke and I'm very tired."

Both of them smiled graciously, murmured farewells, and continued down the sandy path back toward the atrium. By the time I turned back to Dagny, she was running back to the bungalow with one flip flop on and sand flying off her fast heels.

Chapter Fifteen

DAGNY

The world spun around me when I stumbled back to the bungalow, barely able to breathe. My chest had tightened like an elephant sat on it, and it was all I could do to crawl to my bedroom, kick the door closed with a foot, and lay on the ground. The dizzy sensation cleared when I closed my eyes.

Calm down.

Calm down.

Calm down.

The day had been difficult to process without my biological father crashing into me unexpectedly. Kissing Jayson Hernandez was enough to set my stars spinning, and then he destroyed it with a single comment. *It was just a kiss.* Victoria's arrogant posturing, combined with an exhausting dinner filled with small talk, which was my nightmare, left me emotionally depleted.

And to run into Anthony like that?

My chest began to tighten again, but I forced myself to draw in another deep breath. What if Jayson came in? He'd find me sprawled on the floor like a maniac. I covered my eyes with a hand, then scrambled for my phone. I'd tucked it into the pocket of my dress—because Serafina had some magical affinity for dresses with pockets. It's like they *found* her, and she'd given me this one.

Desperate, I sent a quick text into our app.

Dagny: Need you?

Her reply came seconds later.

Serafina: I'm here.

Dagny: Jayson kissed me.

Serafina: WHUT. CALL ME NOW.

Dagny: No. No words.

My breath wheezed as I forced it in and out. The pins and needles feeling in my fingers started to fade, and so did the black halo around the edge of my vision. Serafina couldn't know about Anthony, not with the NDA on the line. But I could get Jayson off my chest. Except no words would come out of my mouth right now. I could barely squeak the breath in and out as it was.

Texting had always been my saving grace.

Serafina: Spill.

With agonizing precision, I texted her all the details of the swim, the body surfing, and then the kiss. It seemed to take forever, and I must have sent twenty paragraph-long texts. But the precision of it helped my body calm and slow.

Dagny: Then he kissed me in. the. water.

Serafina: Shuuuuuut uuuuuup.

A thousand heart-eyed emojis and dozens of others that didn't make any sense followed, like she just banged on the emoji keyboard. Her response, combined with finding the words without my voice, calmed my ragged breaths. The room stopped spinning. My vision came back into focus, and my chest eased off.

Serafina: What a great first kiss story. He always comes through. How are you?

Dagny: Stressed.

Serafina: Why?! He's got the hawts for you!

Dagny: But what if nothing is different when we get back?

Serafina: What if EVERYTHING is different?

My heart gave a little flutter. Everything would be different —for me, anyway. In all the years of my quiet adoration of Hernandez, I'd never considered that we could actually be together.

That dreams could come true.

Hernandez had always been the dream. In some ways, I tucked myself into that imaginary space and stayed there because it was easier than having him . . . and then losing him.

Never had I imagined real scenarios playing out between us.

Real scenarios like what followed after the kiss.

Dagny: But then he opened his big, fat mouth.

Serafina: Uh oh.

Even texting the story helped the night feel better. My fingers gripped the phone so hard they ached, and I was grateful I didn't have to speak. In this state, the words would never come out. Frustration tended to make everything worse.

Jayson had kissed me, then downplayed it once he had time to think it over. Maybe kissing meant something different to him and I made it too big. Perhaps it had just been a spur of the moment decision. A response to the fun.

His comment about what happened being *just a kiss* had shredded me. Before I'd even gone to the dinner, I'd been scrambling for a reason to steal back to the bungalow and gain a few moments alone to think. To not panic. To separate the fear from reality. Victoria's condescension set the dinner off on the wrong foot, and it hadn't improved as the dinner progressed.

Then I ran *right* into the biggest disaster so far.

Serafina: Idiot.

Dagny: Yeah.

Serafina: Talk to him, okay? No assumptions.

I snorted. *Talk* to him? Texting was almost too much. But I knew she was right.

Dagny: As soon as I get my breath and my words back.

Serafina: Get through the wedding first!

I groaned and rubbed a hand over my eyes. The wedding was tomorrow. I had no more mental ability to face a crowd full of people I didn't know, especially not with Anthony at the head of it all. It was a miracle Jayson hadn't hunted me down after running away—clearly something had been wrong. If he had, I'd have to explain myself or pretend I was sick or . . . something. Nothing sounded better than laying on the cool floor and letting my thoughts run amok. I had no energy for anything else.

After a promise to catch her up on everything later, I set aside the phone and stared at the ceiling. With our text conversation, I'd released the pressure of having kissed Jayson Hernandez.

The next fire sprang to life in my mind.

Anthony.

What must I have looked like when we collided, and I looked up to realize *who* he was? My thoughts felt fractured even now as I tried to puzzle that mess back together. Hadn't I crashed into his wife the same way? Perhaps that was my fate with the Dunkin family. Slam into them like a wrecking ball. Threads of my original plan lingered in that idea, but I brushed it aside.

Not anymore. The NDA would stay in my backpack and I'd return to Pineville without another word to Anthony.

Did I imagine it, or did Anthony seem to have recognized something in me? Did I look like Mom, perhaps? Did he notice, like I did, that my nose was an exact replica of his? My hair color so similar? The crash had been fast, but I'd still grabbed onto details that I'd always wondered about. Attached earlobes, like mine. Anthony and I didn't share many obvious traits. I'd inherited Mom's shoulders. Her eyes. No, he hadn't given me much that made me easily identifiable.

Except a stutter.

Speech impediments had some genetic tendencies, or so doctors believed, when so little is understood about the brain and how we communicate. Of all the things I'd never expected to share with my biological father, the multi-millionaire, the stutter was it. What conniving fate gifted me with such a burden from a biological father that didn't want me? Mom could take her universe powers and stuff it.

Slowly, my thoughts gathered themselves back together, and I guided them gently back to Anthony, to what he said, while I stared at the underside of the ceiling and pondered the fact that I hadn't, at least, screamed, "I'm your forgotten daughter!"

A win.

The sound of a shuffle came outside, so I grabbed my phone. How long had I been here? The last text from Serafina had come forty minutes ago. I'd texted her for at least twenty minutes. An hour of just laying here, staring at nothing by the abyss of my thoughts. Jayson must have noticed something cagey in me and gracefully given me time to deal with it.

Too many emotions ran ragged through me to process now. I lay on my side, my body curled in a ball, and watched the stars in the sky through the double doors. A tear trickled out of the corner of my eye, then slid down my nose to plop on the floor. Another followed. I let them go, a sense of release in their presence.

Eventually, my weary eyes closed and I fell into a deep sleep.

* * *

When I woke up the next morning, I lay in bed.

For a moment, my fuzzy brain could only comprehend the roaring sound of waves outside. My thoughts spun until they caught up with the events of last night. Startled, I sat up with a gasp. A blanket covered my shoulders and body. I still wore the summer dress, but my shoes had been set aside and the sand cleaned off the floor where I'd fallen asleep. The thought of Hernandez coming in and finding me asleep on the ground sent a jab of something through me.

Affection?

Terror?

Regret?

Hints of sunlight filtered into the room in bare streaks of color. The brightening horizon lay dark and still against a vague band of black ocean not far away. Waves rushed quietly, a gentle roar that reminded me of a heartbeat. It must be very early in the morning. The rigid muscles that held me upright relaxed a little.

Today, Grady and Helene would officially tie the knot. The official day of Jayson's responsibilities had finally come around, and I realized with another stab of guilt that I had no idea *what* those responsibilities entailed.

Movement next to me caught my eye and I froze.

Jayson stirred on the bed where he lay on his stomach, his face turned away from me. He slept all the way on the edge like he wanted to give me space. He wore an old t-shirt and a pair of basketball shorts, but the shirt crept halfway up his back. I forced myself to look away, but my gaze went right back to the rigid, muscular lines there. I blinked away sleep to study him, startled by his relaxed expression. The blanket he'd draped on me felt soft as I pushed it higher around my shoulders. A rush of warmth followed the thought that he must have been concerned.

I lay back down, the initial rush of panic fading. My half-sleep tangled mind began to clear as I shook the mental cobwebs free. His husky voice followed seconds later.

"You okay, Dagny?"

The question was quiet, a gentle roll. He hadn't shifted, or opened his eyes, or even turned to look in my direction. After so many years at his job, his instincts must have been honed to other people.

"F-fine."

He shifted a little, but still didn't look my way. "I wasn't sure if you felt sick or not, so I wanted to stay with you just in case."

Tears welled up in my eyes, hot and stinging. "Th-thank you."

For a long moment, we lay in the quiet. Finally, he turned his head to face me. Sleepy, dark eyes stared at me for a moment before he broke the lingering morning with another low, rumbled response.

"I made a mistake last night."

My brow dropped.

"What?"

"I made a mistake."

He rolled all the way onto his side, his shirt stretched halfway up his stomach to reveal tight muscles I wanted to run my fingers across. My fingers clenched into a fist and I forced my thoughts to slow.

Was the kiss his mistake?

"Wh-what do you mean?"

Stubble had broken out across his face, darkening his jaw in a shadow. Sleep still lingered in his eyes, which were otherwise bright. My heart beat twice as hard even though I hadn't moved.

"I cheapened our kiss."

The muscles in my face went slack. Before I could express any surprise, he continued.

"I didn't mean to say that our kiss wasn't special or mind-blowing or . . . the first time I've ever really been shaken up by a kiss, which is true. I just . . . you looked so stressed last night. I wanted to take the burden of talking about it off of you until we could both think about what happened without pressure. You're already doing so much for me . . . I didn't want to ask anymore."

Of all the things he could have said, this wasn't what I expected. My thoughts raced to formulate a response, but the ball of guilt that sat on my chest made it slow progress. The balances were tipped, all right, but in his favor.

When I didn't say anything, his jaw tightened. "I . . . I chickened out."

"Wh-what do you m-mean?" I asked quietly.

"I was going to come back and check on you right when we got back, but I didn't. Like a coward, I stayed on my side and gave you space because I knew that I'd made you uncomfortable with what I said. I was trying to help but . . . I made it worse. It's . . . it's like you couldn't get away from me fast enough last night."

He wasn't entirely wrong, but on one hand, he was *so* wrong.

"You are p-perceptive," I managed, just to buy myself time to figure out how to explain the complicated mess this had become.

He snorted. "Obviously not so perceptive, or none of this would have happened."

"I w-wasn't upset w-with you."

"Riiiight."

"Well," I hedged, "a little. B-b-but I ran away b-because . . ."

His eyelashes fluttered as he waited, and a lump rose in my throat. What ramifications could come from me sharing? Would anyone ever know? Hernandez could be trusted to keep the secret, of all people. Hadn't he just proven that?

"I c-can't t-tell you yet, but please t-trust me? It w-wasn't you."

He reached over and his fingers found my wrist, where the tips sat on the sensitive skin where my heart pulsed. He gripped it in a gentle hold.

"Your other reasons don't matter. I'm sorry, Dagny. That was the best kiss I've ever had, and I chickened out and left you alone here because I think I'm falling for you. I think I'm feeling something I haven't felt . . . maybe ever . . . and I don't really know what to do next."

My breath failed completely.

I stared at him as all the blood drained from my face. The casual atmosphere, the easily spoken words. How was *this* a real scenario? He'd told me how he felt like it was so simple. Like I hadn't been harboring my true emotions for years. Like I hadn't dreamed this out time and time again in every different scenario, circumstance, and outfit. He let it roll off his tongue like the truth was so . . .

. . . easy.

A thousand thoughts spiraled through my head in response to his words, but I could only find the strength to form one of them.

"Wh-why?"

He laughed and rubbed a hand over his eyes. Under his blanket, his legs tightened as he pushed them into a stretch.

"Dagny," he chuckled through a half yawn. "You blind, amazing, completely unaware woman. If you saw in yourself what I see in you, you'd never ask me that."

"H-how is this r-real?"

At first, I didn't realize I'd said it out loud until he turned back onto his side, propped his head into his hand, and stared at me with a questioning gaze.

"What do you mean?"

My heart leapt into my throat. Was it my turn to be honest now? He'd laid it out there so casually. Perhaps it was my place to do the same.

But how could I?

Jayson had always lived on the line between idiocy and danger. Dangled in the place where courage was a requirement to survive. I'd never put myself out there like that. So what did it cost him to admit he started to feel something for me? That a kiss was—for once in his life—more than just a kiss? Not as much as the years I'd packed into my infatuation with him. A few days of awareness was a drop against the ocean of adoration I'd given him.

To admit that?

To open that up?

He'd probably be frightened if he knew how long I'd felt something for him and dreamed of his hand in mine. That sort of truth couldn't come too soon, because whatever fragile bloom began would never finish. It was too much. The tidal wave of emotion I'd held back for him would swamp both of us.

I swallowed back a nervous laugh. "Wow, J-j-jayson. I'm . . . I d-don't know what to say."

He grinned lazily. "It's a gift."

"Th-thank you. F-for telling m-me, I mean."

"You're not going to do a whole we're-just-friends, I-don't-feel-that-way spiel, are you? Because there's no way you would have kissed me back like that if there wasn't *something* you felt."

He yawned again as he said it, one hand covering half his face, like he asked that sort of loaded question every day. Maybe he did. Hernandez had always seen the world so differently than me.

If you only knew.

"N-n-no," I said quietly. "N-never that."

He sobered and lifted a heavy, warm hand to my face, where he stroked the edge of my jaw, then let the pad of his thumb trail to my lip. I watched his wrist, too afraid to meet his eyes. He'd see everything written in my gaze. There would be nothing left for me to hide from him if he just saw my eyes now. But I wanted to pull his touch closer. To cling to him and beg him to stay, forever, because the realization of so many dreams was more than I could bear.

"Tell me what to do next, Dagny," he whispered, "so I don't screw this up. I'm sort of new to this and I'm not very good at it. Tell me what you want the most?"

My hand lifted and wrapped around his. He paused, thumb on my chin. I moved his palm so it cradled my cheek and tilted my head into it.

"This," I whispered, "is p-perfect."

Hernandez reached up with his other hand and pulled me into him. I slipped into his warm side and he tucked me under his arm, my head under his chin. The skin of his shoulder burned hot where my cheek rested on it. I hesitated, then let my hand rest on his chest. He played idly with my hair while I closed my eyes.

"This," he whispered, "is why."

Then he pressed a kiss into the top of my head and I melted all the way to my bones.

Chapter Sixteen

JAYSON

Dagny reminded me of a kitten.

Warm, snuggly, but wary at every noise. Last night on the way back from dinner, she'd been panicked, even frightened. The fact that she ran away from me—or perhaps just the embarrassing situation of literally crashing into one of the richest couples in the country—only made the comparison stronger. She was easy to spook and ready to run, tail poofy and mouth hissing.

Now, she purred, snuggled into my side and content. Whatever happened between our kiss and the end of the dinner when I found her asleep on her bedroom floor, I had no idea. But there was also a story deep inside of Dagny that I had a feeling was starting to play out.

My burst of honesty had been selfish. Keeping that crap pent up made me a wild man, because life was too short to mess around with games. If she was interested, great. If not, no problem. I'd come into and out of enough relationships to know most of them just didn't come together.

But Dagny was something else altogether.

Last night while I waited for her to come out and explain

what was going on had been torture. Watching the door. Checking my watch. Wondering if I'd made a mistake in giving her some distance. Then I couldn't handle waiting anymore and I found her asleep on the floor. A single tear sparkled in the well of her eye.

But had that tear been *just* about my ridiculous comment?

I couldn't discount my instincts, which told me that something else was happening here.

Her fingers tapped gently on my chest, almost a song-like staccato, as we lay together in the quiet. The fact that she hadn't run away from my honesty was a win. I'd expected her to friend-zone me and be awkward the rest of the time. What I hadn't expected was a willing snuggle, and it felt like a chance. With Dagny, I had a feeling I'd have to play this carefully and slowly. Despite all the time we'd spent living around each other, I hardly knew her at all.

The insecure tones of her question played back through my mind.

Why?

Why not? I should have countered, and then given her a list of all the reasons why I couldn't stop thinking about her. A list of all the reasons I regretted my obvious blindness for the past how-many-years and why that wouldn't be the case moving forward. Her wide eyes and slack lips had been enough of a reaction. No reason to push her too far now. Let her soak up what I said, think it over, then we'd talk about going home later. For now, I had a wedding to get through.

Yet . . . cuddling her was *way* more my speed, so I'd soak it up for a few more minutes, then try to figure out how to make it happen again tonight. Maybe *after* some of those hot kisses like we had on the beach.

As if she read my mind, Dagny lifted her head. "D-d-do you need to d-do stuff for Grady? C-can I help with anything?"

She shifted, but I didn't let go of the lock of hair that I toyed with between three fingers. A sly grin overtook me—I couldn't help myself. Bastian and I had kept our secret under wraps for so long, there was almost no holding back now.

"You can," I said and stacked an arm behind my head. Her not-so-subtle glance at my bicep, and then quick jerk back to my face, wasn't unnoticed. Would she pass out if I flexed? She looked ready now. The thought almost made me laugh, but I shoved it back. I could torture her later. It would be worth the wait.

"Oh, n-no." She straightened, head cocked to the side. "Y-you have s-something planned. I kn-now that face."

My grin stretched further. "What are you talking about?"

"Wh-what are you doing t-to poor Grady?"

"He has it coming."

"J-Jayson!"

Laughing, I held up two hands in a show of innocence. "Look, Grady tortured us in high school. It's payback time."

"N-nothing to Helene!" she cried, finger jabbing my direction. "Don't you d-dare m-mess with a bride on her w-wedding day!"

"I'm not a monster."

Her expression was far too serious for such a beautiful morning, so I put an arm around her shoulders and curled her back into me. She didn't protest, so I kept playing with her hair. This time, she ran a tentative finger along the edge of my rib. Even through my shirt, it sent lines of fire through me. In fact, it felt far more intimate than anything I'd experienced before. This quiet touch and gentle connection was far more powerful for me than it could be for her. In my world, physical touch often meant danger. Such a calm expression of it healed something hot inside me.

"Wh-what are you s-sup-p-p-osed to do today?"

"Mostly wrangling the other Merry Idiots and getting them places on time. Sounds easy, but it will be like herding cats."

She made an amused sound in her throat.

"The wedding is at 5:00, on the beach near the hotel. Grady and I are meeting at 9:00 this morning to review a few things, then again at 11:00 with all the boys." My lips twitched again. Oh, the anticipation of this day was almost too much. Grady would rue the day he ever decided to let us run amok with a little bit of power. "The bride's luncheon with her girls starts at 11:00, and I think they're doing spa stuff, or whatever. So we're . . . we're having a boys . . . *lunch*."

"Oh d-dear."

She had the right sentiment.

"He'll come back in one piece," I said lightly. "I swear it."

"Sh-she will k-kill you if you m-mess up her wedding."

Although sweet, Helene had a tough streak in her, and I didn't doubt Dagny's prediction for a single second. I released her hair to trail my fingers up her arm, enjoying the silky feeling of her skin under mine. Goosebumps rose under my touch on the second pass.

"Never," I said. "The official *see the bride* moment is at 3:00, and then they're doing pictures until 4:30, then the ceremony. Dinner is at 6:30, and we party all night."

Dagny tensed, but I wasn't sure why. People, crowds, mingling. In general, I didn't have her pegged as a girl that loved that sort of thing. But tonight would be different, because she wouldn't leave my side. And I didn't want to stop touching her, so if she was so easily distracted by my touch now, maybe tonight would be just fine.

"S-sounds like a f-full day. How c-can I help?"

"This is a perfect start. Most of it is me helping Grady. If you want to stay here, I can come back and get you."

"I'm here for whatever you need."

I tightened my hold on her for a moment, and she snuggled closer.

"Thanks. How about you stay here and enjoy your day on

the beach until it's time for us to get together? I'll come back for you after the *see the bride* thing is done and my part in the pictures is over. That'll give you time to get ready and we can head to the ceremony together around 4:30."

She nodded. "G-good."

With my arms braced to hold my weight, I flipped her onto her back and rolled with her. Her breath caught and eyes dilated, but she didn't protest. My fingers tangled in her hair as I studied her, noticing a very light smattering of freckles on her face for the first time. Her gaze dropped to my lips, then back to me. The rise and fall of her chest against mine sent a dizzying curl of heat through my stomach.

"Can I kiss you again?" I asked.

She nodded.

When the soft pillow of her lips pressed into mine, I almost lost it. I scaled back my response, but couldn't stop a low growl. Her hands came around my back as she tilted her head to deepen the kiss. With a sharp breath, I pulled away, then brushed the hair out of her face.

"Touch is a dangerous part of my world," I whispered with a soft kiss to her cheek. "I have to be careful of anyone touching me when I'm on duty, because I never know what it will mean. So your touch is like water to a dying man. Thank you."

Her expression softened.

"And if I kiss you again," I continued in a low growl, "I will not leave this bungalow for the rest of the day. My position as best man is the *only* reason I'm leaving you in this bed alone. I want you to know that."

With that, I pushed away and forced myself out of the bedroom before I frightened her with the raw intensity of what she made me feel.

* * *

At 10:49 am, four DVD's in clear cases rubbed together as I extracted them out of my pocket and glanced at them. Digital copies waited on my computer—I doubted any of us even owned a DVD player—but there was no drama in emailing a file. This way, our childhood and idiotic teenage years would remain truly immortalized through physical and digital means.

In the reflection off the top case, I could just make out my freshly-combed hair and shaved face. My face disappeared as I focused my gaze beyond the clear case and looked at the DVD.

The C-tape.

The stupid camcorder that Bastian found in his father's dinky garage had made us legendary. Not just because of the stunts that circulated on the tape, but the difficulty of finding a VHS. Those who were able to sneak into the library and the old VHS still had been lucky—because many tried, and that old man librarian didn't let anybody through.

Rumors abounded about what stunts we included on the tape, because we couldn't tape all of them. Just the dumbest ones. A lot of the rumors were speculation, but most of it was truth, as dumb as that truth was.

Whenever the Merry Idiots got a new idea, people tried to go with us to see the stunts or predict where we'd act next. For weeks, rumors would circulate until they died down, and we resurrected them with fresh ideas later. Because Vikram was both diabolical *and* popular in high school, he'd throw out ideas constantly, just to keep people waiting. Most of them never happened.

A lot of the time, however, we kept our ideas between us and the tape. Now, the C-tape would see the light of day once again. I shoved all four DVD cases into my pocket and jabbed the elevator call button.

A hand clapped my shoulder as I turned my thoughts away from the C-tape and back onto Dagny. The movement jarred me.

"There's the best man!" a voice cried.

I glanced back to see Anthony Dunkin. Alison, a few steps away, waved over her shoulder and headed to the other side of the lobby as if they'd just split apart. Reputedly, the bride and bridesmaids were supposed to meet there for pedicures before their luncheon.

"Morning, sir," I said.

Although I didn't know him well, Anthony Dunkin had the air of someone that commanded respect, so I slipped into my best behavior voice. The one that even *abuela* received, except I feared her more than the wealthiest man in Texas.

His nose wrinkled, but he had an amiable smile. "Please, don't call me sir. Sounds too much like my grandfather, and I'm certainly not there yet."

"Of course."

His tone turned musing. "How are you these days, Hernandez?"

"Good."

He wore a freshly-pressed white shirt and tie with swim trunks underneath that made me wonder if he'd just come out of a business meeting online. A line remained between his eyebrows, as if he were thinking so hard about something it couldn't go away now. Despite his distracted air, he gave me a warm smile as we waited together. He loosened the tie as we stood there, giving him a rumpled appearance.

"Are you ready for tonight?" I asked. "I imagine it's no easy thing watching your daughter get married."

Anthony blew out a long breath. "Is any father ready to give up his only daughter? No, I imagine I was never ready for this day."

I laughed quietly. "I imagine not."

"Grady is a wonderful man, at least. I don't think I would give her up to anyone less worthy."

"I agree."

A soft, ocean breeze drifted in from an open window not far from the elevator where we waited. The number glowed a bright red 14 now. Upstairs, Grady and the boys waited for me. I was almost late on purpose—I wanted to make sure all of them were there before I arrived. Because once the C-tape was available to all of us again, I wouldn't have the patience to wait.

None of us had seen it in the years that had passed since high school graduation. We'd watched it one last time the night we graduated, then I'd tucked it away until a few weeks ago. Now, I couldn't wait to watch it. To feel the thrill of adventure, the sting of pain, and the swelling of pride.

"So," Anthony said and drew me back. "That girl you brought with you. Dagny Taylor is her name?"

"Yes, sir."

"Lovely woman. I hope you're keeping her close."

"Very, sir."

"How long have you been with her?"

My response stuttered in my mind. Could I lie to a man like him and tell him she was my girlfriend? Wasn't it *Victoria* I was trying to fool? Lying about Dagny felt . . . wrong. Dagny was clean and straightforward and honest and *good*. The things that set her apart from Victoria were the very things I didn't want to create by lying to other people about our relationship status.

Besides, it wasn't about her being the girlfriend. It was about not being single when Victoria was with someone else. But fate had flipped the tables on me. When I returned home, I wouldn't think about Victoria again. I'd be damned if I didn't see Dagny every single day, though. A new fire started in me at just the thought of Dagny. One that so far eclipsed what I once felt for Victoria, it made her look small. I wasn't about to let it die out.

Dagny and I were just getting started.

"What we have is pretty new, to be honest," I finally said.

His brow lifted. "Oh?"

A sweet smell drifted into my nose a second before the

elevator arrived. Someone else stood next to me on my other side in a pair of quiet flip flops and a shimmery, loose dress that slipped around perfectly tanned legs.

"There you are," drawled Victoria, like a cat just waking up from a nap. "I've been looking for you."

She stood a hand's breadth away. She didn't touch me, but she might as well have. Something like the cold kiss of death filled the space between us.

"Hey," I muttered.

Anthony motioned for her to go in first. She obliged, but not before dragging me in with her, our fingers interlocked. When I tried to pull away, she squeezed and held on tighter. Anthony followed us into the elevator, and Victoria's arm slipped through mine.

"So good to see you again, Jayson," she said brightly. "It's like fate just keeps putting us in each other's paths. I can't believe we're about to do this today. Best man and maid of honor? It's like we were *meant* to be together on an aisle. Maybe this won't be the only one."

That cloying tone had returned to her voice again, the one that set me on edge. Whatever she said in that tone before she hadn't meant, because it was the same tone that drew me in in the first place. But I still hesitated in pulling away.

And why?

The question ran through my head, stalling my withdrawal. Stunned by the speed in which she'd shown up and taken command of my thoughts, I just stood there for a moment and said nothing. Anthony glanced at us from the corner of his eye, but kept his head forward.

"Aren't you supposed to be getting pedicures right now?" Anthony asked.

Yes! I almost cried. *Pedicures. Thank you.*

Victoria smiled, her arm tightening around mine. "Yes, I just forgot something in my room and am zipping up really quick."

He gave a kind smile, but his gaze lingered on our arms. Victoria closed the distance between us. I would have stepped away, but that move would have pushed me right into Anthony. Dagny had stumbled all over him enough for both of us. Besides, explaining this odd situation would be even worse, so I gritted my teeth as the elevator slipped higher.

How much longer would we stand here?

There weren't *that* many floors.

This was a small eternity.

"So, Jayson," Victoria said quietly, but with ample strength for Anthony to hear every word. "Tonight, after the festivities have died down, can we meet up in your bungalow again? I'd like to finish our conversation about where our relationship is heading now that we're here together."

The elevator dinged open and Anthony stepped out with a bland smile and a little bow at the waist. His gaze lingered on mine with something like a statement in it. By the time he got into the hallway, he'd pulled his phone out of a pocket and dialed. Even *he* seemed ready to get away from her, his daughter's best friend. I watched him go with a helpless sense of jealousy as the doors slid shut again to take me up four more stories.

"No," I finally said.

Her eyes widened. "You're going to play *this* hard to get?"

"This isn't a game, Victoria. I'm here with Dagny. You and I aren't good for each other. Not even a little."

She frowned. "That can't be true."

"I disagree."

The door dinged again and I stepped out. She followed, then grabbed my arm and jerked me around to face her as the door slid shut. No one waited in the lobby as her fiery eyes met mine.

"This is *not* over," she hissed. "We have only just begun. Our *story* has just begun. Yes, it hit a rough patch, but all the good ones do. You have to believe that, Jayson. *I* choose to believe that."

I paused to study her. Beneath the lines of makeup around her eyes lingered redness. Lack of sleep, maybe? Heavy bags under her eyes, for sure. The bare tone of her voice made her seem stressed or desperate. Dagny, who seemed so bright and fresh and determinedly real, felt like an ocean breeze in comparison to the haggard girl hiding beneath all this fake sparkle.

That's when I knew why I hesitated: because I needed closure. Needed to know for certain that Victoria was the woman I thought.

My tone softened slightly.

"Victoria, for a long time, I was sorry, *very* sorry that you didn't choose me. And I'm sorry that you regret it now. But it won't happen again. Nothing more will happen between us."

Her cold fingers closed around my neck and jerked me down. She laid her lips over mine, attempting to kiss me with passion. Although I wanted to pull away, a part of me wondered.

Was this true?

Had the passion I'd felt at first with Victoria been real?

She pulled away, her breath hitched. Her eyes were inches from mine. "You can't tell me that's not real," she whispered huskily.

I stopped, paused, then pressed one more kiss to her soft lips. They weren't as full as Dagny's. The lipstick left a strange texture, and they weren't welcoming, even though she tried hard to deepen it. I pulled away and waited.

Nothing.

No connection. No sense of vulnerability or adorable uncertainty or even genuine curiosity.

"Sorry," I said quietly. "You're just not the one for me."

I turned and strode down the hall, toward the suite at the end where Grady and my friends waited. My shoes echoed dully as I walked and wiped any remnants of lipstick off my face.

"Jayson!" Victoria cried, her voice shrill. "Stop this madness or you'll never get me back."

I held up a hand as a last gesture of farewell. My card swiped across the door handle and a bright green light illuminated the space above it.

"Jayson!" she snapped. "I'm serious. There will not be a third chance!"

The hotel room door closed behind me.

* * *

Dagny cluttered my thoughts as I strode into Grady's room.

Grady stood near a sideboard of drinks, pouring something into a glass of ice cubes. I clapped a hand on his shoulder and smiled wide as I passed.

"How are you, brother?"

Grady's expression didn't waver. Behind him waited a storm cloud. Bastian and Vik sat on a couch near an open set of double doors that overlooked the sand. Vik had a hot glower on his face. Bastian looked out the French doors, where bright sunshine spilled into the room with blinding force.

"What's up?" I asked.

Bastian drew a finger across his neck, then motioned to Vik with a tilt of his head. Vik scowled at me.

"Shut up, Hernadez," he muttered.

"I didn't say anything."

His frown deepened. "But you're about to, I can tell."

"You're not wrong." I grabbed Grady's shoulder, then shoved him into the couch. "Have a seat, groom." Then I tossed a remote to Bastian. "Pull up the TV, will you? Turn on the DVD player. I have something for you to see."

Grady groaned. "Please tell me it's *not* something that you're going to use to blackmail me later during the best man's speech?"

I grinned as the TV bounced to life.

"You bet I will."

A stormy Vikram and quiet Bastian lurked on the couch as I pulled the DVD up and started the tape. Whatever had happened before I arrived clearly hadn't been good, but this tape would erase all that. The reminder of what we had as friends was all they needed. Besides, this was just a continuation of the tempest that exploded between all of us at the bungalow after we all first arrived.

No more of that mess.

Time to get real.

Seconds later, the initial footage of the C-Tape flickered across the scene. A familiar, although more high-pitched version, of Vikram's voice filled the room. I lowered onto the couch near Grady with a wide smile.

Here. We. Go, I thought.

"Hey!" Vik cried from the television. "Are you ready or what?"

In the present, Grady cursed. Bastian's eyes grew wide. Vik's expression lost the animosity and went slack. He looked at me and pointed to the TV screen wordlessly. I grinned.

"You bet it is," I said. "Now shut up and watch."

On the screen, a small figure lingered at the top of a church steeple three or four stories high. The steeple plummeted down a straight drop, then moved into a gradual curve at the end. The figure on top was me.

I sat there on a rug that I'd turned upside down. Even now, I could feel the pit in my stomach as I stared at that initial free-fall drop before it curved. There were divots to avoid, and it was dusk out. Light enough the video would come through, but not full day in case a cop strolled by.

"No way," Bastian whispered. He shook his head in a half-laugh. "No. Flipping. Way." Vik leaned forward, fist pressed to his mouth. Grady glanced at me, one eyebrow raised in question, but I ignored him and kept my gaze locked forward.

A voice on the screen called out again. Bastian, this time.

"One . . . two . . . go, Hernandez!"

Seconds later, my body plummeted off the top of that church.

My heart did a double beat just recalling the way the rug felt under me as I slid down that metal rooftop. The sense of nothing but air and pain and death beneath my legs for a small eternity—only a few seconds—before I caught up with the part where the roof sloped into a curve. My teeth clenched as I watched it all happen again, without a helmet on.

The anticipated rush of pride didn't follow this video—which was one of my previous favorites. No sense of adventure, nor hope to do even better next time. To get bigger adventures. Top even that.

This time, I could only wonder how I'd survived so many years. What if I'd hit my head? I could have become wholly paralyzed. What would my Mom have done if I had weeks' worth of hospital bills? Surgeries?

"Damn," Vik murmured quietly. "That looks worse than I remembered."

"Yeah," I said.

"Stupid," Grady said. "Stupid, stupid. What if your rug caught on one of those divots? Dude, you could have died."

"We were complete morons," Bastian said.

The video scratched a bit, then turned off. Two seconds later, another one popped up. Another previous classic, with a bright red lobster and Grady's shirt off. The lobster was a few inches away from his left nipple. On the video, Bastian burst out in laughter as the lobster attached to Grady's nipple, and he screamed.

Grady reached over, rubbing it. "Freaking hurt," he muttered.

"Bled like crazy," I said.

We fell quiet, and I wondered why this didn't feel as good as I'd hoped.

Another movie clip started. The smell of asphalt replayed through my mind as it baked beneath my feet on a hot summer day. Verdant green mountains surrounded our teenage selves while Vikram attempted to zipline down a ski lift on a home-made rig. Sparks flew out behind him as he fell, breaking an ankle with the crash of branches and a howl.

Vik hissed and sucked in a sharp breath as he watched the C-tape, then shook his head. His hand massaged that ankle.

"Still hurts sometimes," he muttered.

Grady laughed. "Remember how we tried to splint it with a couple of sticks and some vines? I think we made it worse."

Vik grimaced. "I will never forget that."

Bastian chortled. "Some paramedics we were."

We watched half-heartedly as the rest of the pranks cycled through the tape. Some of them felt childish, like shoving Bastian into a box and pushing him down the stairs. Most of them were dangerous, idiotic. We'd been more fueled by the camaraderie and thrill than the actual tricks, but at the time, it felt like they were everything. It felt like we *were* the tricks. Or maybe we were just notoriety seekers.

By the time the C-Tape flickered off, we'd fallen quiet. The replaying of our childhood idiocy, and the comments back and forth now, came with a mixed bag of emotions.

"Seemed so much cooler at the time," Bastian murmured.

"We were cool . . . weren't we?" Vik asked.

"Just dumb," Grady said with a shake of his head. "Just . . . really dumb. Maybe a little bit bored."

Now it felt . . . crazy.

Filtered through the lens of adulthood and real-world experience, I felt gratitude that no one had died in our ridiculous stunts. After everything I'd seen working at the sheriff's office, the fact that we'd survived had been a literal miracle.

Vik fell into deep thoughts with a frown, his arms folded across his chest. Bastian pulled his bottom lip through his teeth, and Grady just stared at the screen. I pulled the other three copies out of the C-tape out of my pocket and tossed them to each one.

"Had copies made for all of us. So we never forget. Yes, we were dumb. We were lucky to survive long enough that any of us could get married. But we had each other, and that is what really mattered."

A few murmured thanks followed, but I wasn't about to let them off the hook. I pegged a hard stare on Vik.

"Vik, it was good then. We had great times and a tight bond, and our crazy adventures took us down some wild roads. But it wasn't everything, and we can't live that life forever. You see that, right? Tell me you see that that was a different time and we're smarter people now. I need to hear that you can let this go."

Vik glanced from me to Grady, then back to the TV screen, where I'd paused the movie on a shot of the four of us swimming in the water after a particularly long cliff jump that slapped so hard I'd been red for two days.

Vik nodded. "Yeah, you're right. It . . . it was good then. It's . . . it is different now."

I swung my gaze to Grady.

"Grady, don't discount it for what it was at the time. Four idiots that were lucky to survive, but we always had three other people to lean on. Vik isn't upset about losing the danger." I glanced back at him to confirm. "He's afraid to lose us."

After another moment of hesitation, Vik nodded.

"Yeah."

"We all want to stay together." I nodded to Bastian, who nodded back. "But we might need to figure out what that looks like now, as adults. Yes, we may have wives. Grady will have ten kids, Vik will have ten wives that won't ever meet each other, and Bastian will always be frightened of women. Agreed?"

Bastian shot me a glare.

Grady nodded and looked to Vik. "I'm sorry, man. I see it. We're always here. We'll always be friends."

Vik nodded.

I held up both hands. "Great. Now that's over with and we can stop being annoyed with each other, I need to go talk to Dagny really quickly. Then we can get on to this business of getting married, already."

Grady swiped the remote from my hand and shut the TV off. "You can talk to Dagny later." He tossed it back to the couch and pointed to Bastian and Vik. "Right now, we need to go over the ceremony, look at your tuxedos, and get ready for the *see the bride* moment. You good for it, best man? Your girl can wait!"

A lingering challenge lived in that question. This was *his* wedding. Was I going to be the one to mess it up? An itch to tell Dagny about the kiss with Victoria, and how it only made me want her, and things would be different when we returned, reared its head. But it would have to wait.

Properly chastised, I nodded once. He was right. best man duties awaited, no matter how badly I wanted to explain things to her. To tell her that Victoria was a wisp of a dream—but she was the real thing. That boys had to grow up and some women had to go away, but together, we would stay.

Dagny would have to wait . . . at an island resort with delicious food, white sand beaches, and as much sunshine as she'd get anywhere. I had a feeling she'd be just fine for a few hours.

"Of course. We're good," I said. "Let's do it."

Grady grinned in a way that took up his whole face. "Then let's get this settled between me and my wife, y'all. I'm getting *married*!"

Chapter Seventeen

DAGNY

The sound of water slapping the beach reverberated through the bungalow. I stared at the ceiling, half asleep, buried in thoughts of sandy beaches, pristine oceans vistas, and Jayson Hernandez with his shirt off, playing in the ocean.

That would haunt my dream for years to come.

With a little sigh, I shuffled out of the bedroom and into the kitchen. A soft breeze drifted through the room, stirring my hair. I closed my eyes and drew in a deep breath, my thoughts heavy—yet light—with Jayson.

This trip had done exactly what I didn't want—entrench me even farther in my feelings for him. Now, I'd seen a side of him that I hadn't before. The gentle side. The fun side. The side that didn't prioritize danger and drama over safety. Even in Pineville, I saw that same intensity channeled into a different place: safety for others.

Now that I saw *this* side of him, I couldn't unsee it. It made sense, in some strange way, that I should fall harder than ever for him, instead of being more able to let him go. I scoffed when I remembered my plan to see the human side of him and be able to stop my obsession.

That had failed on an epic proportion.

But maybe that was okay. Because hadn't he been amazingly honest? Wasn't there a level of adoration in his gaze I'd never hoped to see?

So why did I still hesitate? Why couldn't I just have some courage and *tell* him already?

While I picked over a piece of toast and some orange juice, my thoughts wandered back to Pineville. We'd leave tomorrow; reality would return. I wouldn't wake up to coconut shell knick knacks decorating the spaces of a gentle bungalow constantly filled with the sound of the ocean. The whir of the Frolicking Moose would take its place. With it came the comforts of the mountains and the dull steadiness of my predictable routine.

Jayson Hernandez might be a more constant part of that routine. I could barely comprehend the thought.

Although I'd been ignoring her so far, Victoria's voice filtered back through my mind. The night of the dinner, she'd acted startled that I'd been attending an online school. As if the position of the school had any bearing on the education that it gave to complete the purpose that I wanted.

A knock at the back of the bungalow drew my attention up. The door was open, allowing the breeze to dance through. A male outline filled the doorway, but shadows prevented me from recognizing him right away. I padded over, feet bare on the wooden floor, and came to a fast stop.

Anthony Dunkin smiled at me.

My heart dropped into my stomach as I reached the door, then paused with my hand halfway there. For a heartbeat, the two of us just stared at each other.

"H-h-hello," I said.

"Dagny." He smiled wide. "Wonderful to see you again. I was in the area and wanted to stop by for just a moment. Do you mind if I come in?"

Warning bells clanged in my head. He gave me no reason to

suspect he was anything but another stutterer coming to talk to someone who could understand, but my hair stood on edge anyway.

"I'd r-r-rather you n-n-not come in-nside," I said.

He shrugged, and to my surprise, didn't seem bothered. "Wise. Very wise. Would you be willing to meet for drinks at the bar?"

"Wh-what does this c-c-concern?"

A smile flitted lightly over his lips. "A breach of contract, if you will. Or, shall I say, a non-disclosure agreement?"

* * *

My heart felt like a lead weight as I mutely followed him toward the hotel bar. I stepped just behind him to give myself a little space to catch back up with the feeling of his stare on my skin. The cat-and-mice way his eyes had studied me. The firmness of his jaw as he'd said the words.

Non-disclosure agreement.

How did he know?

A few people drifted past us and called out to Anthony, laughing as they disappeared into the awaiting sandy beach and palm trees. My palms felt clammy at my side, and a chill had crept through me like a cloud had moved over the sun, but it hadn't. The sky was as bright as ever. The only cloud here walked a few steps ahead of me and hummed lightly, as if he didn't have a care in the world.

He was taking me for a drink, after all. Maybe he *didn't* have a care in the world. Would a man that was truly worried about saving face take me out for a drink? He'd be seen with me this way.

Maybe someone would draw conclusions?

My mind recoiled. No, I wasn't making any sense now. Everything had happened too quickly, so now I tripped over my thoughts *and* my words. Less than a minute later, Anthony opened a door to the hotel and gestured me inside with a grand sweep of his hand. The warmth on his face had me firmly locked in confusion.

Did he know?

Was I missing something?

Back when I planned to confront him about the choice he'd made, I expected frustration, maybe vengeance. But this Anthony was a calm summer breeze. A monster with their prey in his hands, more likely. A pleasant monster, however.

Because *who* had control of the broken NDA?

He did.

We slipped through a hallway of wood with decorative netting and a cool blast of AC. A maid pushed a trolley past with a little smile as the hallway opened up into a ritzy bar. Dark paneling, gleaming wooden floors, and window drapes made from dried grasses left an edge of sophistication on the room. Anthony had to only raise two fingers to draw the bartender's attention, and suddenly we sat in a booth near the back. No one else lingered indoors at this time of day, giving us the shadows to ourselves. Anthony faced the doors while I looked out a window, my back to the room.

The place suddenly felt as small as a cubby hole.

I swallowed past my fear as I gazed across the booth without saying a word, and Anthony did the same on the other side. A waiter set down two ice waters.

"Nothing now." Anthony waved him away with a gesture of his wrist. "Come back in ten, please. Notify my assistant we've arrived."

"You've ar-r-r-rived?" I asked.

"I assumed you wouldn't be comfortable alone in the bungalow, and I try to avoid being in rooms with women that aren't my wife."

The response, spoken with an undertone so blatant I could have swam in it, set me on edge.

Was *I* the lesson that spurred that decision?

Once the waiter faded away, our eyes locked. Some of my courage had returned in the minutes between then and now, when I realized this would not be a friendly, happy reunion. Despite his genial air, he sat like a coiled snake. Tension hung across his shoulders and arms. Likely, there wouldn't be pride or astonishment or even rage on his features once we established what we each knew. At best, I could hope for indifference. A father-daughter reunion of bland annoyance.

My heart gave a little tremble, but I forced courage into it. Not much remained, but just enough for now.

"Dagny Taylor," he murmured. A pleasant expression remained on his face, but I could have sworn I saw a sense of shock beneath it all. Perhaps curiosity.

I nodded once, then endured his business-like scrutiny. As if confronting me for the first time, he studied my face. I could feel his eyes mark my nose, my ears, my neck. The perusal felt mostly benign, likely the same thing I did the other night. At one point in my life, I'd imagined our first meeting to be something like this. The search for touchpoints or physical similarities between us. I'd longed for a biological father that wanted to share something with me, even if it was mere physical traits.

"You look nothing like me."

"I d-d-disagree," I murmured.

One eyebrow tweaked up in a move I couldn't read at all. Was he startled? Or was the stutter simply a reminder that we did share something after all?

"There are so many questions that I have." He leaned back, and I sensed a poker face at work. The man was one of the wealthiest in the country, which meant he was going to be better at this than me. Over all the years of hopes and dreams, I'd tied myself up into this outcome too much.

Meanwhile, I doubted he had thought of me at all during that time.

Wordless, I motioned for him to continue. He released a breathy laugh. "You've learned not to speak unless you have to, I presume?" He shook his head, as if he didn't really want an answer, but felt obligated to ask anyway. "I know that struggle well. All right then, ask I shall."

His hands folded together in front of him. For a moment, the intensity of his gaze deepened, then abated.

"What is your favorite color?"

I blinked, entirely unprepared for so benign a question. *Why are you here?* or *How did you find out?* made far more sense. Even *how much money do you want in exchange for your silence?* wouldn't shock me.

But this?

"G-green."

"Really?" He grinned. "Intriguing. And how is your mother doing?"

My nostrils flared, but someone had appeared that drew his attention away and he missed the tell. I took the opportunity of his distraction to square my shoulders and draw in a deep breath. One of my speech therapists said that just drawing my shoulders back could give me the courage I needed to open my mouth again.

Still, a sense of astonishment filled me. He was asking about my Mom?

A familiar-looking person appeared. A young girl, presumably his assistant, handed him a large, sealed envelope. Once he accepted it, she disappeared again. He slid a finger under the top and glanced to me.

"Your mother?" he asked in a gentle reminder. "I hope she's well."

"F-f-fine."

"Good. And do you like the mountains of Pineville as a home? You've been there for so long."

"Y-yes."

He nodded, then reached into the envelope and extracted a sheaf of papers. "I'm glad to hear it. You seem healthy, bright, and intelligent, which is what I wished for you. Now, I assume you have many questions."

The papers spread out in front of him, but the words were too small to skim or catch quickly. I had a feeling he knew that. Maybe this was just a distraction—a preface. He made polite small talk now, but in his hands he held a bomb.

"C-can we s-s-stop the s-small talk?"

Anthony paused, hesitated, and let out a sigh that lowered his shoulders. "Of course. It's not small talk to me, as I've genuinely wondered about you from time to time, but I can see that it is for you. Let's get to the bottom of this, shall we? You hold some information about yourself that you shouldn't, technically, know."

Although I didn't know much about this kind of back-and-forth, I at least knew that I didn't have to verbally admit anything. What if he recorded this? No, that didn't make sense either. He wouldn't want his own voice on the recording as he admitted an affair and a secret love child, at any rate. I stared at him, my lips sealed.

He paused for just a second, as if to give me a chance to reply, then continued again.

"The information you learned about yourself has explosive potential. Not only would it dramatically affect my personal life, but the lives of those I love and have long been loyal to. Right down to the employees that depend on my company to feed their children. It's a long tail of success, you see."

A scoff slipped out of me, and I didn't try very hard to stop it.

He blinked. "I deserve that from you," he said quietly, then put both hands down on the papers to stare at me again. This time, his expression was . . . softer. The kind of gaze a father *might* give a daughter. "When you bumped into me the other day before I made it back to the rehearsal dinner, I almost thought I'd seen a ghost. You look just like your mother did twenty-some-odd years ago."

The edge inside me started to soften. Although I wanted to act indifferent and as if I didn't care, I couldn't help but cling to the wistfulness in his voice. Hadn't I dreamed of this moment my whole life? I'd tried to imagine what he'd say about the decision to leave me behind and ignore me my whole life. He left a big, fat question mark in the place of a father.

Now he handed the answers to me in a gentle tone. One that even seemed to have a hint of regret in it.

Was the regret for me?

"You weren't a ghost," he continued, oblivious to the way my mind swam around from hope to despair. "You were just a spitting image of your mother."

"You r-r-rememb-ber her?"

"I do."

I frowned. So did he. "Perhaps not on purpose," he amended, "and not with the best of feelings. What happened between the two of us wasn't her fault alone, and I don't blame her. But it certainly wasn't an action I can say I'm proud of now."

The sincerity in his tone took me off guard. I couldn't help the way his words made me feel: unwanted and betrayed. He flicked the words off his tongue easily, as if he didn't care about what they really meant.

Was I the action he wasn't proud of? No. I was the result of it. His adultery led to an out-of-wedlock child. Breathing proof against his worthiness to such a lovely wife. Likely he regretted outcomes more than actions. I kept those thoughts close.

"Regardless." He shook his head and rubbed a hand over his

eyes, the first sign of humanity I'd really seen. "I saw you and wondered. You fit the age. You had a stutter. When you saw me, you looked as if you'd seen a ghost, too. You looked the way I felt. So I sent a message to my investigator and set him off to do his thing last night."

The pieces clicked into place. So he had recognized me, then learned whatever he could. Although weird things happened every day, it seemed almost impossible that I just *happened* to come to the island where my biological father threw a massive wedding event for his daughter.

Not his *only* daughter, however.

Had fate thrown this together? Some great, cosmic force that rolled the dice when our lives decided lessons?

"And?" I whispered.

"And he confirmed you as . . . well." Anthony cleared his throat, but his drawn gaze eased a little. Even *he* wouldn't say the words, and that hurt. A diabolical insult to my existence. A reminder of who I would always be to him. "The confirmation was an odd feeling. I can't say I was surprised. As I mentioned, you look just like your mother. But I was . . . concerned."

For the first time, I could see that my presence must feel like a threat to him. Did he think I came to unravel everything? To enact revenge or justice? Because he would have been right . . . at least initially. But now everything had changed again.

Perhaps he was being so pleasant now out of fear of reprisal. Even a hint of scandal at a time and place like this could unravel his daughter's most important day.

"I'm n-not here for t-trouble."

He smiled, but clearly didn't trust me.

"No one ever is," he said blandly, then tapped the papers below his hands. "Whether your mother told you about the situation, whether you found the NDA, or something else doesn't matter. It's clear you know what has happened between your mother and me? Do you deny this?"

My hesitation came because for the first time I realized that this whole trip was, in the heart of it, a basic assumption. Did I *know* that the NDA was Mom's? That they'd had a one-night stand? No. The idea was based on pieced-together ideas that I'd cobbled together out of tenacity and desperation.

The moment I'd seen him standing alone on the back porch, it's like I'd realized the truth. Anthony Dunkin, oil tycoon from Texas, really *was* my biological father. His arrival on my doorstep confirmed it.

Although the paperwork that existed had pointed that way without question, having him stand before me now made it undeniable in my heart. Something in that positive confirmation sent my soul into a spin, like doors slamming shut.

"I d-d-don't know for sure," I said. "I've operated l-largely on an as-s-sumption."

"How so?"

"I f-found the ND-DA. Sh-she doesn't know I kn-now."

"Did you look for me?"

All my life, my heart whispered.

"Af-fter I saw it, I was c-curious. I G-googled you."

He stared hard at me, gaze tapered, then nodded once. "Interesting," he murmured. "Well, I've come to present you with a proposal of your own."

"B-but—"

He held up a hand, and I stopped. "Please," he said, "allow me to get through this explanation, and all your questions will be answered."

Reluctantly, I nodded.

"Below me is a contract not unlike that I gave to your mother. It details what you cannot say. To make the explanation simple, there would be nothing you can say about my name, my business, or any relationship with anyone in my life. In other words, I do not exist to you."

My throat thickened. With every word that he said, his voice became more firm. There was an odd, melodic sort of rhythm to his words as he slid away from Father of the Bride and into Oil Tycoon. Reality crystallized with every passing second.

This man wasn't my father and never would be. Not in all the ways that actually mattered.

Although thirsty for his attention and interest in me—even the morsels he'd tossed my way with humanizing questions—I'd exposed myself to a new world of pain. Just entertaining his presence set me back. He'd been kind at first. One could even call him interested. But his interest wasn't in me, our shared genes, or our history. His interest was in self-preservation.

Cruel, I thought as he spoke quickly and succinctly of the terms of a contract that prevented me from ever returning to any property that he might own, or speaking to any media or news outlet in terms that threw any suspicion on him, his business, or his family. He'd pretended to be a friend, had maybe even held some level of curiosity for me. But now he'd become an intense businessman focused only on the outcome.

He's not my father, I thought.

Cotton filled my mouth when I asked, "And w-w-what if I d-d-don't sign?"

He smiled a little, and I thought I saw a snake in it. "That is an option, but not one I'd recommend."

"W-why?"

"Your admission here makes it abundantly clear that your mother broke the NDA. Perhaps unconsciously or passively, but it *is* broken. The repercussions are astronomical to her." He gestured to the papers. "Built within this agreement is an assurance that your mother will receive no consequences for breaking our NDA, provided she continues to keep it. Since she allegedly doesn't know that you have seen it, then we will continue keeping her under the same illusion as before. Provided you agree with the final terms, let us get this signed."

He reached into his jacket and pulled out a pen.

My chest filled with a cold breath as I stared at the metallic sheen of the pen that found itself into my fingers. Disbelief followed my shock, which seemed to just be catching up with me.

What had I been thinking?

To come to this island in pursuit of a biological father that clearly wanted nothing to do with me. Only ghosts and broken dreams and lonely nights waited down the road of my parentage, and maybe I knew that when I started this journey. But I'd chased it anyway, because at least in the pain there were answers. The questions could be silenced, and all the other questions that had arisen could be dismissed as mere ghosts now.

The pen hovered over the paper as my mind continued to spin.

"W-what is the f-f-final c-condition?"

"You leave now."

My head jerked up. "Now?"

He punctuated his response with another nod. "Now. I have a private plane that's waiting for you. It will take you back to your life in Pineville where you can resume with the monetary compensation outlined in these pages."

My eyes grew. "B-but the wedd-ding. J-j-jayson."

"Jayson." He sighed. "Yes, Jayson."

The silence hung there for a moment while I sorted through what he asked of me. It was more than just leaving him to his secrets. It was leaving Jayson here without explanation. Without one *ever*. The contract meant I couldn't tell him the sordid history that lay at my back, and he wouldn't be able to trust me ever again.

"I-I can't leave h-him without t-telling him g-g-goodbye and explaining," I protested. "Th-that's not f-fair."

"You're sure he's worth your mother's well being?"

"Y-yes," I said without hesitation.

He scoffed.

"Y-you would f-f-force me into that ch-choice?"

His gaze returned to mine, and I almost thought I saw sorrow for a moment. "For the sake of everything I love and own," he said quietly, "yes."

My heart ached as if a cold hand had seized it. Maybe in different circumstances, I could have grown fond of Anthony. Could have enjoyed the idea of him living out such a privileged life with his wife and his daughter and the grandchildren she'd undoubtedly give him. But his superiority, selfishness, and utter disregard for his own choices made it impossible for me to respect him.

Mom, however, shouldn't have to pay the price.

"And you are a-a-able to s-sleep at n-n-night?" I asked with a snap of pain I couldn't hide anymore. "Y-you c-can look at your l-l-lovely wife in the eyes and kn-now what y-you've done?"

I wanted you to love me, I thought. But the words would forever remain behind sealed lips.

A gaunt expression covered his face for a moment. He ran a tongue over his teeth and, for a moment, seemed to consider something. Then he pulled up a phone and typed something out.

"I'll never give you what you want from me, Dagny. But I can give you one thing. Give yourself a moment to think this out while I make a call."

My chest shook like an earthquake as Anthony pressed the phone to his ear and walked just out of hearing range. He kept me within his eyesight and blocked the only exit with his body.

Shakily, I looked down at the contract. The words blurred together at first, and I had to read the first line several times before it came into focus.

The contract seemed meticulous, although I had no expertise in this world. Most of the words went over my head, and I thought of Kinoshi, the town lawyer in Pineville. He'd have plenty to say, I would bet. Even Maverick would be better to judge this than me. But there was no help. I had to figure this out and move forward.

By the time I read through all five pages, my mind had turned to slush. A monetary figure stood out amongst the sea of letters at the bottom, near the word *consideration*.

$500,000.

I blinked and stared at it.

Half a million dollars. To him, I had a feeling it wasn't much. Perhaps he had a way to act as if it were a tax write off, or something. But to me, that could be the start of my new life. The life I hadn't been able to visualize without the goal of tracking down my biological father and finding a way to talk to him. With it I could buy a house, start making some investments, and pay off debts. Whatever I wanted, and wherever I wanted it. Money mixed with plans and sound financial sense meant power and choice.

Anthony returned a heartbeat later. I glanced up, startled to see him there. He slid back into the seat with what could have been called a warm smile, but I knew better. Anthony wasn't warm *anything*.

"Forgive me," he said pleasantly, "I had a call to make about something. This, in fact. Before you hesitate to go home, I thought you might like to see this. Taken just before I arrived here, in fact."

He slid his phone across the table. A black and white video was paused on the screen, and my heart gave a little *thud* when I recognized Jayson. Then, next to him, stood Victoria.

Something cold trickled through my body.

"Go ahead," Anthony said, with the tone of voice I would imagine a cat had before it caught a mouse. "Play it. Let's see what happens."

Although loath to play into the trap, I couldn't help but tap the triangular button in the middle of the screen. A security tape, clearly, of the inside of an elevator. A date and time stamp across the top recorded it as only a little while ago. No sound came with it, but I didn't need sound to understand the way Victoria had a possessive hold on Jayson. Anthony stood next to them, and even I could feel the tension in the air.

"I-it's an elev-vator ride," I murmured.

"Keep watching."

The video ended with them stepping off the elevator and onto another floor. Immediately after, another video popped onto the screen. This one covered the hallway outside the elevator, but from a different angle. It had panned back, but gave a clear view of the two of them as Victoria hauled Jayson into a kiss. My stomach caught painfully, but I kept my expression neutral. Jayson looked tense. The kiss wasn't long *or* soft. More forceful and . . . forced.

"This is—"

"Keep watching," Anthony sang.

Then Jayson reached down and kissed Victoria.

This was slow, a little lingering, before he pulled away. They were only a few inches apart as they spoke about something, but I couldn't read the signs. Was Jayson passionate or upset? The angle was bad from the side. They didn't stay there long, eventually parting in different ways.

"That," Anthony said quietly, "is the man you're waiting around for, isn't it? Better just to let him go on with his life, don't you think? Sometimes, we have to let paths go to embrace what truly waits for us. Just like your mother did."

Just like your mother did.

Is that the path that truly waited for her? Or was it the path that Anthony Dunkin shoved her onto through his inability to keep his pants zipped?

A bubbling emotion I could only identify as rage built

within me. Or maybe it was thwarted, feminine power directed at Jayson. At Anthony. At Victoria for speaking down to me because of my stutter and kissing the man I had hoped for for so long. But waiting and hoping were just a waste of time.

"So," Anthony drawled and pulled my mind back to the moment. "The contract. Have you had a chance to review it?"

For the sake of surviving the moment, I turned my mind away from Jayson—he'd get his turn. Now, I had to deal with Anthony.

"Y-yes." I cleared my throat.

"And?"

My thoughts whirled as I reviewed a way to respond to the $500,000 consideration attached to such an outrageous contract. The terms were exorbitant, paranoid, and a little . . . unstable.

Anthony, no doubt, wanted me to believe that he'd attack me and my Mom with all the power at his disposal should his secret ever go public.

But *would* he?

Right now, I was beholden to no such NDA. So, any power play against my mother was easily within my reach to shout from the rooftops. Yes, he'd pretend that he would attack in court . . . but could he afford to? A paternity test was all Alison needed to show proof of who her husband *really* was. Although I'd resolved not to involve Alison or out Anthony, now I felt no such restraint. A letter, left discreetly somewhere. A tip that someone she loved received from an anonymous source. Or perhaps an article blasted all over the newspapers and internet.

No, he approached me like this because *I* had the power.

Not him.

If he were to punish my mother, I'd fight back. That's why he wanted to do a separate agreement. Why he played so softly, but carried a stick that could, if I let it, wallop me to the ground.

My heart raced as I set the contract pages down and stared at them. Never in my life had I truly exercised courage. Never had I stood up to the bullies. Never had I told someone the way I *really* felt.

That time had come.

The papers gathered together under my fingers. I stacked them on top of each other and slid them back to him.

"I w-won't s-s-sign it."

His expression fell into one of mild confusion, but he didn't seem altogether *that* surprised. Instead, he lifted an eyebrow.

"Oh?"

My throat had turned dry, but I swallowed past it and forced myself to meet his gaze. The tightness in my chest tripled, but I breathed through it. My entire body felt oddly calm. Powerful.

Courageous.

"You h-had your ch-chance to exp-plain," I said. "N-n-now I g-get mine."

He hesitated only a second before he leaned back in the chair, then motioned for me to continue with a wave of his hands. I drew in a stabilizing breath, prepared to do the sing-song that let me get through something without the stammer. If there had ever been a conversation made for it, it was this.

"Ten years ago, I helped my Mom clean out her closet. She's a bit of a h-hoarder, but that's not important. A small folder tumbled out of a box while she was in the other room and I found it there."

The breathy tones of the song, and the weird way I had to string my words together made the retelling feel a bit unnatural, but at least the words moved out of me now. They spilled between us like forgotten secrets, and I didn't want to stop them. His brow furrowed. I had his whole concentration.

I shook my head with a breathy, sardonic laugh. "The NDA hit me like a meteor in the chest. Mom rarely spoke about you. Said I was the result of a weekend fling and we'd never see you again. No names. No dates. No facts. Nothing. Then, the NDA dropped into my lap. Of course I searched for you afterward so I would know the man that agreed to act as if I didn't exist or matter."

Here I stopped to draw in a breath. Emotions lodged in my throat, the ones I didn't want him to see. The ones he hadn't *earned*. He didn't deserve to know that I'd been curious about or yearned for him and his acknowledgment of my existence. But I couldn't help it, because some barrier in my mind had broken, and all the words I'd never said flowed out of me like a river.

"I found you so easily. You were wealthy. Apparently happy. With a beautiful daughter and wife and house as large as anything I'd ever seen." I scoffed. "Or s-so it seemed. I . . . I couldn't help but wonder if one day I could just see you up close. *Speak* with you. I dreamed of outing you and forcing you to acknowledge that I exist. That I matter too. Then, Jayson told me about a wedding that he wanted me to attend with him. The wedding of a girl I'd never heard of until he said her name. Your n-name."

My strength faltered, but Anthony didn't move. He sat there, frozen on the bench. The bar at our backs lay almost totally empty except for the distant shriek of someone outside, and the drone of the TV. He gave no indication that he understood what I was saying, just sat there like a statue.

Undaunted, I pressed on.

"When he said your name and that you'd be there, I couldn't help myself. I'd worked *so hard* to earn money to find you. To . . . to s-scrape together s-something! Whether I wanted to admit it or not, I d-deeply desired a connection to you."

My voice elevated so fast that I clamped my lips shut to temper it again, then met his gaze and kept going. I leaned forward, hands on the table, and unleashed all the intensity that still made my bones tremble even now. As if revealing my truth brought it about with even greater strength.

"I saved every last dime I had because I wanted to fly to Texas, stay in a hotel, and concoct some way to meet you. But

Jayson gave me a way to save the meager amount I've been able to hold onto while paying my way through college and w-working at a diner and a coffee shop. So I came. And I saw you. And if you hadn't approached me, I would have left this island without saying a word to a single soul. All I wanted was to *see* you."

His throat bobbed as he swallowed. Too hot to quit now, I kept going.

"Do you know why I would have left, silent as a tomb? Because never in all my life have I ever felt such deep disappointment over another human being. You're materially successful, wealthy, and have the most beautiful family. You don't deserve a single part of it. I don't want my name to be associated with you. Anthony Dunkin, you are a failure in all the places that matter, and I hope it haunts you to your dying d-day."

The table groaned as I shoved away from it and stood up. I towered over him, seething with righteous fury now.

"I will not sign your contract and I will not take your filthy money. You can come after my innocent, kind mother if you like. She has never broken her part of the agreement, and she never will. She will never know that I sought you and that I found you. But I will be under no such restraint. If you so much as take her to court over this, your name and the paternity test in the NDA paperwork will be spilled over every single news outlet in this country. And if you think I come from a small town and don't have the connections to make that happen, you're denser than I expected."

My leg shuffled back a step. Anthony hadn't moved a single inch. His entire body radiated tension as he stared at the spot where I had been sitting.

"Your secret is safe with me, Anthony Dunkin," I hissed. "B-because you are the l-l-last p-person I w-w-would ever want as my biological father."

With that, I turned and stalked out of the bar with my chin held high and my heart finally galloping free.

* * *

Tears streamed down my face when I stumbled back into the bungalow. I slammed the door shut and locked it. Then I rushed from door to door, window to window, locked all of them, then stood at the kitchen sink and slowly sank to the floor.

Sobs shook my body as I let the tears free. Years of questions had just been satisfied—and so painfully. Years of hope were destroyed. Shredded. Torn apart. All the time of wondering and waiting and thinking.

Poof.

Gone.

While I vented all the locked emotions, the warm island air built up in the bungalow until it felt sticky with heat. I welcomed the physical discomfort as a distraction, but eventually, all of it was swallowed up in sheer despair.

An eternity later, I unwound myself from the ball I'd tucked myself into and lifted my head from my knees. The unmistakable smell of Jayson Hernandez slammed into me then, and I recalled that I was back at our shared bungalow, which carried his scent.

I had another monster to face.

Victoria.

With the blurriness that emotion brought to memories, I recalled the security camera. The uncertain lines of tension in Jayson's body. Unmistakably, he *had* kissed Victoria. Did it mean anything? The forming fissures in my heart meant that it likely *did* mean something, but I didn't know what.

All of my life I'd dreamed of Jayson Hernandez. Drawn strength from the idea of him that had, somehow, played out in real life. Never had I actually thought that the real Jayson

Hernandez so closely resembled the one in my head. Now, that man may have just thrown himself back into Victoria's arms.

And whose fault would that be?

The heat of our shared kiss on the beach had been real. Dazzling. Like a firework in my blood. I hadn't imagined it out of sheer desperation. No, he'd kissed me like he meant it, and that meant I still had a chance.

So I needed to find out.

With the back of my arm, I mopped up my tear stained cheeks and slowly stood. If Jayson really had gone back to Victoria, that was his choice. I'd work through my pain and eventually wish them both well, but I wouldn't figure it out by sitting here on the floor.

Now, I had to take this as a chance to do what I should have done years ago. But no matter how I looked at it, this confrontation was far bigger, scarier, and offered more devastation in my life than anything Anthony Dunkin could have brought.

This time, I would finally tell Jayson exactly how I felt.

Chapter Eighteen

JAYSON

Bastian clapped a hand on my shoulder, his face illuminated by a wide grin. "Grady," he whispered, "is going to destroy you for this. I can't wait."

I laughed quietly, my shoulders shaking with delight. "It's his own fault," I murmured. "Grady left his *see the bride* moment wide open."

"I can't believe Helene agreed."

"She'd be crazy not to. This will be hilarious."

Ten steps ahead of us, Vikram sashayed barefoot down a sandy trail in a hideous white wedding dress that Bastian had bought from a thrift store on his way here. Wrinkles from being shoved into a bag creased the fabric, and it smelled like campfire. The sleeveless top, shaped like a heart, left his broad shoulders bare. Chest hair puffed out over the top. Gauzy fabric rippled around his knees as he hurried through a lush garden set in the hotel grounds, away from the sounds of revelry near the beach. His bottom lip was split and swollen after a wrestling match between him and Bastian on a surfboard got too out of control.

In other words, he was the ugliest bride ever.

Ahead waited Grady, his back to us. A sleek tuxedo fitted all the way to his wrists and made his shoulders as wide as a refrigerator. The photographer had been talking to Grady, but she stopped and stared at us as we approached. Her lips rolled together to school a laugh. After Grady said something to her, I thought I heard her say, "Oh, don't worry. You will *never* forget this moment."

Grady expected to see lovely Helene, dolled up with all the thousands of dollars that her father could throw at a team, waiting for him.

And he'd get *us*.

Vikram slowed, half-turned to give us a thumbs up, and faced Grady again. The photographer swallowed hard as she turned to Grady, camera up and at the ready. Her lips twitched.

"Are you ready?" she asked.

A body moved behind the photographer, phone raised to record as a video. Tyrone, Grady's cousin. He kept his expression even, but the hilarity already rang in his eyes. Grady opened and closed his hands at his sides, a sure sign he was nervous.

"Can I turn around now?" he asked quietly.

The photographer nodded. "See your . . . bride."

The word came out a garbled, poorly suppressed giggle. Grady whirled around, expression eager, and then stopped. Vikram held out his arms, a cheap bouquet of twigs and grasses in his hands, and cried, "I do!"

Grady's face fell into a mixture of horror and astonishment. Bastian and I fell to the sand, howling.

"What the hell?" Grady cried.

Vikram threw his arms around Grady's neck and tried to get Grady to carry him. "Marry me, lover boy!"

The photographer snapped away, tears streaming down her face as she laughed. Bastian doubled over while I tried to catch my breath. The expression on Grady's face slipped away from confusion and into a wary amusement.

"Grady, man." I wiped tears off my cheeks. "Your face."

A slow smile worked through his terror at seeing Vikram half-naked, his hairy legs sticking out of the skirt which was a foot too short. Grady started to laugh and the rolling, reverberating sound didn't stop. It grew in intensity until he struggled to stay upright.

Bastian hooted. "That was worth the entire trip alone. I can't believe that was so worth it. Grady. You're a mess."

"So dumb," Grady cried, but slapped Vikram on the shoulder as he wiped tears out of his eyes. "So dumb."

Movement shuffled behind Grady, but he was too distracted to hear the whispers of sound. I struggled back to my feet, my sides aching, and clapped Grady on the shoulder to keep his attention on me. While a vision in white appeared from around a fence, I kept my hand on him and sobered.

"You got this, my friend." I gave him a big smile. "She was made for you."

Grady's smile dropped into question, then his lips rounded into an O. I motioned with a nod behind him, where Helene now stood in an ivory-colored gown, her shiny hair swept away from her face and lips bright red.

"She's there?" he murmured.

I nodded. "Good luck, brother."

Grady hesitated, gave me a nod, then turned. The photographer crouched down, then snapped a picture the moment Grady's face went slack and he registered Helene standing there. Her dress cascaded to the sand in a waterfall of white, brightening tanned skin and eyes that sparkled with tears.

Grady's lips dropped open, his brow grew heavy, and his eyes began to shine. He lifted a hand to his eyes.

"That's my wife," he whispered.

Helene beamed, one hand held out. A sparkling, diamond bracelet clasped her wrist.

"That's your wife." I shoved him toward her. "Now go get her, you Merry Idiot, before I take her away."

* * *

A text chimed on my phone half an hour later as I walked through the hotel foyer, my part of the wedding photos finished. One hour until the official ceremony, and I still had to finish my best man speech. That would come. I'd figure out something on the fly.

I pulled my phone out of my pocket, then grinned as I read the message.

Grady: Thanks, man. Good times. I'll never forget it.

Jayson: We always got your back. Always.

Grady: Merry Idiots forever.

Jayson: Forever.

With a chuckle, I shoved the phone in my pocket and turned toward the bungalow. My thoughts moved to Dagny, then Victoria. A new eagerness to see her propelled me faster, and I gave into a slow jog. I just wanted to see Dagny. Let her know how I felt about her and what happened with Victoria. We had a little time before the ceremony, then lots of time after to get the third kiss out of the way.

First, I'd broach the topic slowly. Talk about her day, see how she'd spent the time, compliment her dress for the ceremony. Then I'd tell her the way I felt. That I'd been an idiot and we'd lost so much time. Why hadn't I seen her? Why hadn't I noticed her in Pineville before now? I still didn't have a good answer, even though I'd been mulling it over in my head for days now.

Once we discussed my idiotic ability to see what was right in front of me calmly and rationally like adults, then we'd get to the business of forgetting Victoria and discussing how much better life in Pineville would be with Dagny at my side. At least, that's how I wanted it to go.

We'd see what she had to say about it.

The waves welcomed me and my tangled thoughts as I turned down a sandy path that led to the bungalow.

Halfway there, I skidded to a stop.

Dagny stood a few steps away, frozen with one foot a few inches in the air, as if she were taking a step forward. Her eyes were wide and red-tinged. Her cheeks had a warm color over the tan skin. She wore an elegant black dress and carried a pair of creamy heels. Her hair tumbled around her shoulders instead of tucked away from her face with messy pens.

In a word, she was exquisite.

To my mind, not even Helene rivaled Dagny right now. My breath caught. For a moment, I thought I understood a little of Grady's emotion. His possessiveness. The way he chose Helene above all others without a moment of doubt or hesitation. Seeing Dagny there, looking so frightened, vulnerable, and uncertain left no doubt in my mind.

For her, I'd do the exact same.

Fear pooled in my stomach for a moment before I forced it to calm down.

"Dagny?"

She blinked several times, then swallowed.

"Are you all right?" I asked.

She nodded.

I ventured a step closer, suddenly uncertain about myself. She had that doe-like wariness to her, like she'd dart away the moment I twitched in a way she didn't like. But why? Why had she been crying? What made her so upset? She attempted to hide the tear trails, but I could see the evidence in her open gaze.

"I'm an idiot," I blurted out. "I'm a total idiot."

The uncertainty in her expression dropped. "Wh-what?"

In two steps, I stood in front of her and had her hands in

mine. Her fingers were cold despite the perfect warmth of the day.

"I'm an idiot." I licked my lips and squeezed her fingers tighter. "All the years that you've been in Pineville and I've been *totally* oblivious. I—"

"Stop."

Her firm command, without stutter, startled me into silence. For the space of a breath, we just stared at each other. My heart did a somersault. Oh, no. Had I read this situation totally wrong? I took my shot and now everything was going to plummet downhill from here. My mouth opened, then closed. I didn't know what to say.

"I n-need to g-g-get this out f-first. I n-need to b-be b-brave. B-before you . . . b-before you say all the r-r-right things."

My confusion deepened. "What?"

"I l-l-love you."

My heart dropped all the way to my feet. Astonished, I stood there and stared at her. *I love you* wasn't a trite expression from someone like her. She pulled away, fingers fidgeting, her teeth worrying her bottom lip. But she didn't look away from me. Nor did she hide her soulful intensity.

"I've a-a-always l-loved you," she continued. "Ever s-since my first d-day as a f-f-freshman in high school, when I s-saw you walking down the hallway with the other M-m-merry Idiots. I f-felt you in my soul, and then I spent the r-rest of my life building up a p-picture in my head of who I thought you w-would be. Of . . . how your k-k-kiss would f-f-feel. The heat of your hand in m-mine."

Her fingers closed together, and she grimaced a little. When she closed her eyes and drew in a deep breath, I wanted to ask her to breathe for me. Because I couldn't. The enormity of what she said was almost impossible to comprehend.

No way.

How had I missed this too?

A stupid, lopsided smile crossed my face.

"Really?"

Her painful expression deepened into a grimace. "R-really," she whispered. "I-I've never b-been able to g-g-get you out of my h-head."

My mind raced through the few blatant memories that I had back in Pineville. Mostly of her at work, every now and then out and about her life. Quiet. Shy. Calm. But her gaze had been attentive, which I'd always dismissed as nervousness from my law enforcement uniform.

Maybe it had been something else.

"All those nights at the Diner?" I asked quietly.

"Y-yes."

"The coffee shop?"

She recoiled a little, her voice a calm whisper. "Yes."

"You felt something for me all this time?"

Astonishment stained my voice, and I wished I could take it back because Dagny paused, her jaw tight. As if it made her more uncomfortable for me to be so shocked. How could I not be? Words failed me, and I cast around uselessly for something to say.

Something like determination built up in her eyes before she tilted her head back, lifted her chin, and said, "Y-yes, J-jayson Hernandez. I-I've always c-cared about you. C-couldn't g-g-get you out of my head. A-and that's the full truth. S-s-so you have it. I w-want you a-and a part of me always w-will."

I took another step toward her, but she didn't seem to notice. She barreled into whatever she'd come to say next.

"If you w-want Victoria, th-that's . . ." She swallowed, as if she couldn't get the words out. Seconds later, they spewed out like a volcanic eruption. "Th-that's your i-idiot choice. B-but I couldn't l-let you d-do it without knowing that I . . . th-that I loved you."

Her eyes turned stormy, and I wondered if she recalled our

kiss on the hot sand and cool surf, just like me. If she remembered the warmth of having someone at her side, the way I felt. The way I couldn't wait to learn everything there was to know about her.

My hand reached up to brush the skin of her face with the back of my knuckles. Her eyes fluttered closed.

"Why do you think I want Victoria?"

With a guilty little look, she said, "You k-kissed her outside the el-levator."

I recoiled. "Were you there?"

"N-not exactly," she muttered wryly.

My brow furrowed. How could she possibly know that? I dismissed it with a little shake of my head. Details could come later. For now, I needed to ground into whatever we had unfolding right now.

"I had to know." I shrugged. "When I kissed you in the ocean the other day, something . . . it was so different. Victoria's kiss was cold and forced and hard and it didn't make me feel anything. But I had to know that I was over her."

"Are you?"

"Yes." I laughed. "I'm not even sure there was anything there to begin with."

Her head tilted down as she seemed to consider that, betraying a fan of dark eyelashes against her skin. I put a bent finger under her chin and lifted her head. Her eyes closed.

"Dagny?"

"J-just s-say it," she whispered. "W-whatever you're g-going to say."

I leaned closer, until my face was a breath from hers. She hadn't opened her eyes, but her breath hitched. She held it, her heart pounding so hard I could see it at her graceful collarbone.

"I don't want Victoria," I murmured. My fingers slid into her hair. A tear dropped out of her eye and I swiped it with my thumb. "I want *you*. That's what I came to tell you. That I've been an idiot all this time. The perfect woman was at my finger-tips, but I never saw it."

I caught her sob with a kiss.

Her warm, gentle lips met mine. She threw her arms around me with a cry, then melted into my touch. I kissed her breathless. I kissed her until my chest burned with the force of my heart. I kissed her until everything inside me was about to explode.

Before I could say a word, she buried her face in my neck with a little cry. I crushed her too much, stunned by the feeling of her body pressed to mine.

DAGNY

The wedding moved past me in a gentle blur.

Jayson held onto my hand as he gently led me onto a sparkling dance floor in the middle of the hotel atrium. Other couples quietly swayed around us to a violin-led slow song. The room had been dimmed for the father-daughter dance, during which Anthony Dunkin appeared unwell, and pale, and left the room as soon as it finished. Once the ceremony was completed, Jayson had taken my hand again and wouldn't let it go.

Meanwhile, my brain operated with bright, flashing lights.

JAYSON HERNANDEZ LIKES YOU.

JAYSON HERNANDEZ LIKES YOU.

His many, stolen kisses lingered on my lips like a secret breath. Even the way he held me close, his arms wrapped around my body so possessively, sent my heart into another flutter. I could hardly comprehend what he had said to me. What *I* said back. The gumption it required of me to lay it all out there after years of adoration. To put my heart on the line and watch it chug away, into someone else's hands.

Jayson's hands.

Almost a decade existed between the awestruck freshman

that fell hard for Jayson Hernandez and who I was now, but the giddy joy of young love had seized me all over again. Only this time, it was better. More complete and loaded with time and experience.

"Dag?" he murmured.

I tipped my head back to look at him. He studied me, as if trying to make sense of all this, and my lips split in a wide grin. The tip of his fingers touched my cheek, and a slow smile filled with adoration followed. He looked at me the way I'd always looked at him. My brain nearly split in half with the attempt to comprehend.

Jayson. Hernandez. Liked. Me.

He pushed a strand of hair out of my face. "Thank you for coming with me."

"Th-thank you f-for inviting m-me."

"You know it was my pleasure."

We whirled in a dizzying circle, and I laughed as I clung to him. A shout across the room caught my attention. We glanced up to see a worker from the hotel escorting what appeared to be a bouncer across the room, toward a sloppy-drunk Victoria. She clung to her wine glass and growled as they approached. They spoke quietly and pointed toward the door, but she resisted with a firm shake of her head. Then reached back and grabbed the table to stabilize herself.

"B-b-bit too much to d-drink," I murmured, although I couldn't deny a thrill. Finally, I wasn't the one wallowing in sadness over Jayson Hernandez. While I felt a pang of sadness for her—even commiseration, because I knew how it felt when Jayson didn't know I existed—I couldn't help my relief.

This time, I had the one I wanted.

"She has a lot to be sad about," Jayson said, then whisked me away into the dance again.

When the dance ended, he cupped a hand around my cheek and pulled me into a sweet kiss, then let me go when a wolf whistle came from behind us. Bastian and Vik approached, their neckties loosened and shirts untucked. Jayson drew me into his side, an arm around my shoulders, as if the other two would start a tug-of-war.

Bastian winked at me.

"Finally!" Vikram rolled his eyes so hard his head tilted back. "Has he *finally* figured out how hot you are?"

Jayson growled. Vik laughed and held up his hands in a gesture of surrender. My cheeks brightened in a blush as Vik laughed it off.

"Calm down, calm down. I'm not making any moves. It's just been obvious for a while that the two of you would be a great fit. Dagny was always checking you out." He sent me a mischievous grin and Jayson muttered something unintelligible under his breath.

"You s-survived," I said to Vikram.

He grimaced. "Just *seeing* the altar made me want to vomit. Standing next to it is a bit too close for comfort."

Bastian whistled low. "Too close for comfort."

"W-w-where's your c-computer?" I asked, and realized this was one of only a few times that I saw him without it. An adorable little blush appeared on his cheeks.

"Excuse us," Jayson said before he could reply. "But I have a sunset to watch with my girl. We'll be back."

Jayson squeezed my shoulder, then led me out of the atrium and into the cool, fresh air outside. The sun had almost disappeared into a watery horizon, leaving ripples of color on a calm ocean. Wordless, he led me farther down the beach until we stood with our feet in the gentle surf. Water played at our ankles with a gentle hiss.

"P-p-perfect," I whispered.

The shifting colors of the sunset, and the star-studded sky that followed, sent my heart into a little twist of disbelief. The gentle breeze cooled my skin as we stood there, close to each other in the quiet roar of the surf.

"Just like you," he murmured.

He pressed a lingering kiss to my cheek. Behind us, the wedding party collectively laughed as the dancing shifted into a brighter song. Jayson had already finished a hilarious and historic best man speech. Most participants were warmed with champagne and wine. A buffet dinner would be served soon, and the night's festivities would continue uninterrupted. Meanwhile, my pattering heart held onto every moment as the most cherished memory.

Goodbye, Anthony Dunkin, I thought. He didn't deserve my hope. Nor did he deserve Helene, Alison, or the accolades of his peers. But most importantly, he didn't deserve me—and he'd never have me. That honor was reserved for people like Jayson, who earned it through his compassion, care, and openness.

This was the perfect ending to the old Dagny. To my old hopes, dreams, and life. No more clinging to a man that didn't want me in his life. Now I had Jayson Hernandez, and I had a wide open horizon at my feet.

The best new beginning.

The stars thickened overhead. A brisk wind shuffled by. Jayson held me closer, talking quietly about things that didn't matter, but the rumble of his voice in my ear was like a song. I sank into him, grateful that the dream had come true. Even though I'd just closed a big door, a brighter future awaited.

And I couldn't *wait* to see what it would bring.

Chapter Twenty

DAGNY

Serafina: Isn't it great when Prince Charming finally comes?

Her text put a huge smile on my face.

Dagny: Definitely.

Serafina: Just wait. It gets better every day.

The tinkle of a closing door filled the Frolicking Moose.

I glanced up, then grinned a second before a warm pair of thick arms wrapped all the way around me. Hernandez swallowed me into my favorite bear hug. The force of it slammed my back into the closest wall, but he cradled the jarring motion with his hands. Then he pushed the hair out of my eyes with one hand and kissed the breath out of me. Before I could give as good as I got, he nuzzled my neck, then sighed. His weight sagged against me like a bag of sand.

I set my hands on his back, grateful to feel his warm, reassuring heat against mine. "Bad day?" I asked against the rough skin of his neck. Happiness streaked through me as I drew in a deep breath from his shirt. Even though he'd just gotten off a shift, he still smelled like that spicy mix of outdoors that I loved.

"No."

"T-tired?"

"Not really."

"N-need a little love?"

He growled into the hollow of my neck. "From you? Always." He leaned back, eyes bright. "Oh, *abuela* wants me to ask when you're going to be back. She's making her favorite tamales for you."

"T-tomorrow?"

He shook his head. "Not soon enough. She wants you tonight."

"I was j-just there l-last n-night!"

He shrugged. "*Abuela* gets what she wants."

"I-I'll be th-there."

"She likes you better than me," he mumbled.

Laughing, I pulled away and shot him a you-better-behave glare as a customer approached the store from outside. He stayed behind the counter as two college-aged men strode inside. He moved a little closer and cast a stern gaze on them.

"They aren't g-going to eat m-me," I muttered under my breath. "C-calm down."

"Maybe," he drawled. "Maybe not."

When the two college students proved they wouldn't leap across the counter and endanger my life, Jayson backed away as I completed the orders. He sat at his usual table and watched me work. Once I finished, he beckoned me with a hand. I grabbed his favorite mug, already filled with black coffee just the way he liked it, and joined him. He pulled me into the bench next to him and linked our fingers together.

We talked about his day. My day. The way fall was giving way to winter, and snow flurries were expected tonight. The conversation was punctuated by bursts of chilly air outside when new customers slipped in.

"How's the last class going?" he asked as he finished off the last of his coffee.

"B-beautifully. On t-track to graduate in D-december."

"We should have a party."

"Oh?"

He fingered my left hand ring finger but said nothing. I stifled a smile. Hernandez liked to pretend he was so macho and quiet and secretive, but he sucked at it. He'd been eyeballing my ring size for weeks now.

I had no doubt that a *graduation party* might also end up being an *engagement party.*

Whenever it happened, the day that Jayson proposed to me was the day I would tell him about Anthony. Rage-fueled or not, I *had* made a promise to Anthony that I wouldn't betray. No one would know about my parentage. But neither would I keep a secret from my husband. So once Jayson tethered himself to me that way, I would tell him.

And I know he wouldn't care.

"Your Mom good?" he asked.

"Yeah. Got her new grinder in, so she's happy."

"Still trying to source bee pollen?"

I tilted my head back and laughed. "She is. You wouldn't believe the weird conversations she's having with people."

He grinned. "I'll call her tonight about the shelves in the garage. Just about done putting them up, then she can store some of that stuff in there."

I smiled adoringly at him. "Thank you."

"Oh, the Idiots are getting together next month. Going to start a yearly retreat."

My ears perked up. Something had happened at the wedding to pull the Merry Idiots back together. Jayson didn't go into details, but I had a feeling he was responsible for it. Whatever it was.

"Yeah." He grinned. "We'll take turns being in charge. Vik is starting it off. He wants to do an arctic expedition with sled dogs."

I burst out laughing, then sobered when Jayson didn't follow suit.

"Is h-he s-serious?"

"D-dead serious."

"W-will you g-go?"

"You bet I will."

With a sigh, I laughed. "Of course you will, and I can't wait to see the pictures."

Just as he stood up to leave, and I twined my arms around his neck while the shop lay quiet around us, the door banged open. Two bags made a *thud* as they dropped to the floor. I whirled around to see a woman with black hair standing there. She pulled aviator sunglasses off her face, set her hands on her hips, closed her eyes, and drew in a deep breath.

"I'm back!" she cried, then spun to face me with a tilted smile.

"Ellie?" Despite obvious joy on her face, I thought I saw a hint of exhaustion. I straightened up. "You're b-back?"

She grabbed her aviators and flung them onto the counter. Like she'd planned it, they slid to a stop just before the edge.

"College is done. I'm out of that alcohol-ridden, controlling, exploitative rats nest."

"That good?" Jayson quipped.

Her expression dropped into a dark scowl, highlighted by the light color of her eyes against her ebony hair. "No, I didn't even make it a full semester. It's not a safe place and not a good fit for me."

Jayson held up two hands. "I agree, my friend. I did community college and then joined the force."

Ellie relaxed slightly. Concern filled me as I studied her. Lines edged her face, which had thinned out since she left two-and-a-half months ago. My mind filtered to Devin Blaine, her best friend. He'd left last year and she hadn't seen him since. Their falling-out had been epic news around the town for a while. Although she tried hard not to be, Ellie was transparent as glass. She'd planned to go to the state university *with* Devin. Her attempt now had been a chance to prove she didn't need him.

But she did.

The two of them were fire and ice, but somehow they'd made it work. Devin was gentle, patient, and calm. Ellie was intense, fierce, and prone to isolating. She'd never been the same without him, and I couldn't help but wonder if she saw that.

"I'm onto my next *real* adventure," Ellie declared. "I tried college. They failed me. I'm out." She cut her hands horizontally. "I am *done*."

"So what's your next adventure?" Jayson asked as he wrapped an arm around my waist. Ellie grinned with a fiercely feminine gleam in her eye.

"I'm going to be an adventure guide."

Note From The Author

Regarding the C-Tape—yes, it's real.

It actually *was* a VHS put together by a bunch of danger-loving teenage friends of my brother. He never participated in their antics, but he always talked about them. Of course, rumors of the C-Tape swirled through my life from several different people and places. It really was legendary in my Idaho town, and their stunts actually happened.

These teenagers were not called the Merry Idiots, but probably should have been. Nor were they baseball players in a mountain town, and their names are not used here. They were a pretty tight knit group of boys that, to my knowledge, are still friends today.

It's unlikely that these boys (who somehow survived to become men) that created the C-tape will ever know about this book. It's even more unlikely that they'd know me by my married name because I rarely interacted with them. In fact, I was more like Dagny and in awe of them as a whole.

To the original C-Tape creators: if you do find this book and you recognize my name and some of your foibles as I glorified them in this book, then know that I dedicate this book to you and all your idiotic—but hysterical—ideas.

You awed a little girl that listened from the sidelines.

To everyone that helped make this possible, *thank you so much.* I appreciate all the beta and sensitivity readers that helped me create the best possible story for you, and on a tight timeline! My team, my readers, my family, and all the people that help me navigate my daily life so that I can get words on paper—you are so appreciated.

Wild Child

A SNEAK PEEK INTO THE 6TH BOOK.

The smell of alcohol stained the air.

Grimacing, I hovered around the edges of a crowd of sweaty high school bodies clad in elaborate, strappy dresses and tuxedos. Hairspray and perfume thickened the air. A simple dress of deep blue rustled around my legs with no design except a layer of sheer, shimmery fabric over the top. The bodice was a little tight, but my chest felt tight anyway.

Anyone would, wearing a *dress*.

Not to mention the fact that I hadn't been asked to this prom. My best friend was here with the sweetest, most popular girl in the school, and I hated crowds with an introvert's fiery passion.

Still, I pressed on.

The high school gym hadn't truly transformed despite the sparkle lights, food table, and crepe banners clogging the air. You can't hide run-down with cheap decorations, not even for the last dance of the year.

The sudden absence of pulsing music left shuffles and whispers in the air. The principal, Mrs. Comstock, tapped across a stage on the far side of the gym. She wore a pair of bright pink high heels and a pencil skirt of sheer black. Teenage couples pulled apart, turning their attention to a spotlight that illuminated her salt-and-pepper hair pulled back into a bun, as she stopped at a microphone in the middle of the stage. She held an envelope in her left hand.

"Boys and girls," she said, voice fuzzy from the speakers. "Hope you're having a good time, and thank you for behaving yourself. The time has come to announce the King and Queen of this year's prom."

A round of applause and whoops rippled through the room, followed by a drumroll from the DJ, who worked in the corner. My stomach clenched. As if any of them needed Mrs. Comstock to tell them who would be King and Queen. I crossed my arm in front of me, tucking my icy fingers away. At least I wasn't late.

Where was the perfect couple, anyway?

My heart thumped as a familiar set of broad shoulders came into view on the other side of the room, near a punch guarded by the towering football coach Mr. Bell. He glowered behind the bowl in a challenge to anyone who tried to get past him with alcohol. Not far from him, my best friend Devin had his hand around a girl named Cassidy's. He tugged her closer to the middle of the room, where a few of his football buddies had congregated. When Devin leaned down to whisper in her ear, and she grinned broadly, I clenched my fingers together and resisted the urge to dart away.

This was a mistake. I shouldn't have come. Didn't matter that it was Devin's senior prom, that he'd surely take the crown with Cassidy, or that it was our only opportunity to have a dance together before we exited the teenage world and stepped into the adult one.

I shouldn't have come.

But something—maybe innate loyalty or a deep desperation

—kept me glued to the spot as Mrs. Comstock ruffled through the envelope to pull out a piece of paper. As if everybody didn't already know the two names there. Soft music started in the background, a royal accoutrement with dramatic violins. Two of Devin's friends nudged him from behind. A good-natured roll of his eyes followed.

I wanted to vomit.

Mrs. Comstock leaned closer to the microphone, gazed out on the crowd, and grinned. The spotlight washed out her tanned face as she waited to delay the suspense. Somewhere in the crowd, a girl tittered. Another called out, "Just say it already!"

My heart hiccuped as she paused for another seemingly endless minute before crying, "Devin Blaine and Cassidy Tanner!"

Music crashed through the speakers, drowning out the shouts and cries of almost everyone in the room. Devin, with a heart-stopping smile, held a bent elbow out for Cassidy. A hand covered her mouth. Her eyes—so perfectly warm and kind and compassionate that I wanted to hate her but couldn't—sparkled with shock.

Really? I wanted to say. *You're surprised?*

The perfect couple ascended the stairs on the side of the stage together, toward the awaiting student body president and vice president who held their crowns. Cassidy's tiara sparkled obnoxiously as they set it on top of her head. She looked beautiful, with her dark skin and bright eyes offset by an aquamarine dress. She waved at her adoring public that had gone wild the moment the crown hit her head.

But it was Devin that took my breath away.

The tuxedo cut angular lines across his thick shoulders, and his hair had an adorably tousled look. Star quarterback had served him well—he looked like a king up there with his bowtie, wide smile, and a genuine affability that boggled me.

I leaned back against the wall, crushing my skirt in my hands. My heart banged so loud in my ears I couldn't hear the congratulatory screams anymore. Just the race of my blood through my body. There was only half an hour left of the dance, plenty of time to find him in the crowd later and fulfill the promise of our dance. Cassidy would let me—she was good and kind that way. She wouldn't think that the tag-along best friend who was only a junior would be in her way.

Because I felt like she was in *my* way.

An ugly truth had occurred to me as I'd watched him get dressed for the dance. The moment I comprehended the pit in my stomach at the thought of him with another girl. Seeing him on the stage, as far from me as he'd ever been, slammed the truth into me all at once.

I freaking loved my best friend.

Now, watching them dance and whirl together, the truth was confirmed. Devin had always been more than a friend to me. He was my soul. He was *all*. Tears pricked my eyes with heat and I forced them back with one last shot at my crumbling denial. No. I couldn't love Devin. Not like *that*, anyway.

Devin was my best friend, not my lover. He was the other part of me. The second side of my heart that beat in tandem with mine. The last seven years living in Pineville, away from the stepfather that wanted to kill me, had been bearable because of Devin. Amazing because of Devin.

Safe because of Devin.

"Dammit," I muttered as the weak strands of my denial began to fade. Why did I even try? There was no denying the truth.

I *did* love him.

And how could that ever work? It couldn't. Because love was fickle and men left. Even the ones you loved. Mama had made that lesson very clear.

You fall in love, she told me, *and men leave. It's the way of things for girls like us. Besides, baby, you're the kind of girl that will always take care of yourself. You deserve the truth from your Mama, because I'll tell it to you straight: Stay away from them.*

Never mind that Mama had had some weird views on life, and had led my older sisters down terrible paths with her advice. While Mama whispered sweet tales of romantic passion to Lizbeth, she told me the cold hard facts of life and love. Men leave. Love fades. Take care of yourself first.

Jim, my abusive stepfather, made it very clear that I wasn't good enough for him. And my real father had left me to die with Jim. While I had glowing examples of worthy men—my pseudo-father Maverick, my brother-in-law JJ, and of course Devin—the truth always rang in my ears like a high-pitched reminder.

Men leave.

Love dies.

You take care of yourself.

So, no. If I loved Devin and lost him too, I'd lose myself. Was it worth the risk? Well . . . maybe. Because wasn't Devin already inextricably tied up in me?

Besides, I thought as I watched him and Cassidy twirl around the stage to an especially pungent romance song, *Devin deserves the princess, and I am the sword maiden.*

Dev and I were too alike.

It would never work.

That felt easier. Brutal, cold hard reality. Not the dreams of me being the girl in his arms. Me in the tiara. Me in the dress— and actually enjoying it, which would never happen. No, this was reality, and reality was far safer than dreams.

With all my strength, I swallowed back my emotion. Pushed back the truth that had dangled at the edge of my mind for years now. Even though I'd only just acknowledged my feelings for him today, I tucked them in a tiny box and set it in the corner of my mind to ignore. There they would pulse like a little heart, reminding me that they knew the truth, even as I strove to live a lie.

The crowd surged into the dance as Dev escorted Cassidy off the stage. Suddenly, my tendency to keep to myself and ignore almost everyone but Devin swamped me. There was no one else here I knew aside from a few acquaintances who waved in the halls. No reason to stay. Stay and dance and tell Devin how I really felt?

No thanks.

Locked away now.

A tap on my shoulder distracted me. My shoulders bunched as I whirled around, then they relaxed. My only other friend, Jax, stood there with a wry smile.

"Ellie?"

"Hey." He tilted his head to Devin. "How you doing?"

My tension faded. No punch in Jax's hand. No alcohol on his breath. Instead, I swallowed and said, "Great. Just wanted to see it happen."

"You knew they'd get it?"

"Who didn't?"

He grinned. "They look great together, don't they? The two nicest people in the school deserve the crown." His eyebrows rose. "Don't you think?"

"Yep."

"You all right?"

I tilted my head to crack my neck. The room felt like a warm swamp filled with cheap perfume and alcohol. Mr. Bell abandoned the punch bowl to escort a kid out of the room by his shoulders. Two other kids slipped up, emptying a new bottle of what appeared to be rum inside the punch with a snicker. Idiots.

"I'm good."

He nodded knowingly, as if I'd said something wise, but I

caught the hint of sarcasm in his face. "Sure. You're good. You just got here?"

"Yep. I'm on my way out now."

Wrinkles appeared in his brow. "Why? Don't you want to dance with D–"

"Nope."

"Ellie—"

"You look handsome tonight, Jax." I patted his lapel, where a red rose graced the pocket, "I need to go."

His gaze darted behind me, then his lips twitched. I sensed someone approaching as Jax stepped back a little.

"Good luck with that," he sang. A second later, a hand grabbed mine. I whirled around, coming face-to-face with a grinning Devin.

"I *knew* you'd come."

My heart stalled like a dying star. I sucked in a breath to get it going again, arrested by the overwhelming presence of Devin, my best friend. The guy that was usually sweaty, smelly, and fell asleep with his body half on top of mine most Friday nights while we watched zombie movies. The guy that made a mean grilled cheese sandwich and never had a sip of alcohol just for my sake.

The little box in the corner of my brain exploded open.

Somehow, I managed a smile. "Hey."

As easily as breathing, he tugged me closer, put his hand on my waist, and whisked me onto the dance floor. I caught a quick glimpse of Jax over Devin's shoulder as I whirled away. Concern waited there. Before I could figure it out, Devin spoke.

"So . . . you came."

An undercurrent of joy infused his words, not to mention surprise. A moment of annoyance washed through me. Of *course* I came. But I let it go. Parties were not my thing and he knew that. His words were a comment on my loyalty for him, in a roundabout way.

"Of course," I said quietly.

I couldn't look him in the eye. For the first time in my life, I didn't see the muddy little boy that caught fish with me. I saw Devin the young man. The graduating senior. The man who planned to work a filthy construction job for the next six months until I graduated early and we moved to the state university together.

If he looked into my eyes, he'd see it all.

The utter vulnerability of my feelings took my breath away. Still, with his smell banishing the trace amount of alcohol in the air, I couldn't help but relax. This was Devin. Devin was home. Even in a crowd of people that thought me reclusive and strange, Devin was safety.

Devin was my best friend.

"You looked great up there," I managed to say. "Cassidy is beautiful. So . . . congratulations?"

He made a noise in his throat. I risked a quick glance up and couldn't help a laugh when I saw his crown. Up close, it appeared cheap. A pliable metal with laurels and berries on it, sprinkled with green glass gems that mimicked the school colors of gold and emerald.

Devin smirked. "Laugh it up," he muttered. "I can't wait to take this thing off. Will you have food for me when this finishes? I'm taking Cassidy home as soon as it's over, and then I'll head your way. I'm freaking *starving*."

"You ate like three cheeseburgers three hours ago."

"I know! And I've been dancing and talking all night. That makes a man hungry."

Suddenly, I really relaxed. The irony in his voice. The ease of his escape to me. Even if I wasn't Cassidy, I still had Devin. Stalwart Devin that never changed, that I trusted with every morsel of my body.

"Of course. All the bananas, fudge, and ice cream a high

school quarterback could dream of. Bethany just went shopping and also bought your favorite pizza rolls and bread."

He pulled me a little closer. I closed my eyes as we moved together, breathing in his scent. I'd hate myself for it later, even as the gentle hint of pine lifted from his skin. We'd gone on a hike before he left to pick up Cassidy. I could still smell traces of the outdoors on him.

"Thank you," he said quietly and I knew he meant for coming. For braving a crowd with hidden alcohol that made me extremely uncomfortable. For venturing out in a dress, with my hair freshly washed and straightened. For being here with him on this transitory moment, even though I didn't have to be. I should have been flattered, but instead I felt scared. His breath was hot on my neck and sent a shiver down my spine.

"Of course," I whispered.

His hold on me tightened. My temple pressed to his jaw. Could he feel my heartbeat? Did he sense how breathless this made me?

"There's something I wanted to tell you tonight," he said.

His voice turned down slightly. With the music still blaring around us, it was almost imperceptible. I thought I imagined it. But then his palm turned clammy against mine.

"What's that?" I asked. My voice was a rasp, but he didn't seem to notice. The slow song shuffled into another one.

"I, uh, received some news earlier today. Good news, but it will surprise you. Maybe not really news. More of a confirmed decision?"

He became a rigid board around me as he rambled around a blind topic. I blinked, fuzzy with the sense of impending doom. Of everything about to change. Of the world sliding away from me like a mudflow. I didn't even have to speak. He'd paused for a beat, then plowed forward before I could tell him to just spit it out already.

"I enlisted, Ellie. I've joined the Marines. I leave for San Diego in two weeks. Two days after I graduate."

We were too close together for me to see him, but I didn't need to. The steadiness of his voice, slightly hushed around the edges, let me know he was scared. Scared of what I'd say. How I'd react. We stopped dancing somewhere near the edge of the gymnasium, not far from a bright green EXIT sign.

I've joined the Marines.

It echoed through my mind with undulations. For half a breath, I almost laughed. Told him that it was a funny joke and the timing was poor but the rigid way he held me in his arms—almost like he didn't *want* to see my face—told me this wasn't a joke.

He had joined the Marines.

"What?"

"Ellie, let me explain before you run off, okay? It's . . . it's the money. I can't afford to go to college, even if I stay home for six months and work and save it all. The scholarship I was hoping for didn't come through."

While he continued to explain, the words filtered through my mind. *GI Bill* and *no stress about finances now* and *we'll be okay* vaguely occurred to me. My mind narrowed into a fuzzy tunnel of thoughts that all revolved around one tiny phrase. It whispered through my thoughts in Mama's voice.

They always leave.

Heart thumping, I pulled away. A panicked expression filled his face, but I didn't look right at him.

"I-I need to go."

Before he could protest, I headed toward the glowing sign and pushed through the heavy doors. It spilled me into the parking lot, and the cool air from late spring shocked me out of the tunnel. Out of the questions.

Out of disbelief.

While I stumbled toward the truck, the door slammed open

against the wall behind me, then wheezed closed again. Footsteps ran to me.

"Ellie!"

He reached for me, but I moved my arm too fast. Livid, I whirled around to face him. This time, I looked him right in the eyes.

"How long have you had this planned?"

He faltered for only a moment. "Since last summer."

"Last summer?" I cried. "That's over a year."

Uneasy now, he nodded.

"Last summer is when we started talking about going to the state university together. When we *toured* it together. Do you remember that? Do you remember us discussing plans and talking this out and you agreeing?"

He shifted. "Ellie—"

But I plowed over his plea, too hot to stop now. "Did you know then that you wanted to go to the Marines?"

"I don't *want* to Ellie. I just don't have a choice."

"Did you know?" I asked again, my voice expanding.

His jaw became rigid as he stared at me, so gorgeous in the low light that it made my heart ache. Finally, he looked at the ground and nodded. His voice was low when he whispered, "Yes."

"Yes you've been lying to me for a year?"

His nostrils flared. "Yes, but—"

He stopped on his own this time. When he finally set his eyes back on mine, I had to look away. There was pain and fear and disappointment and maybe, just maybe, a hint of resentment. It was that chance of resentment that sent a shockwave through me.

I stepped back, shaking. Another tremor of pain crashed through me. *Resentment.* Was I holding him back? Did he feel trapped with my friendship? There was nothing else to do. I had to escape. Had to leave. Had to get out of here before I . . .

Exploded.

"Okay," I whispered.

"Okay?"

"Okay."

What else could I say? For the last year, Devin had been sneaking behind my back, letting me believe we had a future together. All that time, he knew he would betray me to go to the Marines. He allowed me to believe in the dream of us.

And isn't *that* when I'd fallen in love?

When the thought of it being just him and me wasn't a dream? When we'd leave this small mountain town and conquer the world? When everything wasn't so scary and so big and so impossible because he would be at my side?

And it was all a lie.

The heat in my eyes returned, this time with ferocity. Still, I blinked the tears back with the maddening thought that Mama had been right. Although I'd talked myself out of believing her for the last couple of years because Devin was different, Mama had been absolutely right.

They always leave.

Maybe it was just a matter of time for *all* of us. For Maverick to leave Bethany. For JJ to escape from Lizbeth. Maybe we all ended up alone.

Safer that way, at least.

"Ellie." He put a hand on my shoulder and I realized I'd stopped moving away from him to stare at the ground. "Please tell me what you're thinking. I know you feel betrayed and this is frightening and . . . "

He trailed away again. My heart fought my head which hurt from all the pain and everything felt like a big, ugly trap that rolled around me. And, pulsing in the corner of my mind, was the tiny box where I'd tucked the truth and it screamed at me now.

You love him. You love him.

And now?

He's leaving, Mama whispered. *Because they always do.*

I stepped back. "I have to go," I said. "I . . . I have to go."

With that, I picked up the dress that I'd carefully chosen, grateful that I'd worn my tennis shoes, and I disappeared into the night with a carefully masked sob.

* * *

Visit www.katiecrossbooks.com to buy your paperback copy today!

Also by Katie Cross

The Health and Happiness Society

Bon Bons to Yoga Pants (Lexie)

I Am Girl Power (Megan)

You'll Never Know (Rachelle)

Hear Me Roar (Bitsy)

What Was Lost (Mira)

The Health and Happiness Society Collection

Finding Anna

Coffee Shop Series

Coffee Shop Girl

Lovesick

Runaway

Fighter

Shy Girl

Wild Child

Smoke and Fire

Clean Sweep

Protect Me

Katie Cross is ALL ABOUT writing epic love stories and wild places. Creating new books is her jam.

When she's not hiking or chasing her two littles through the Montana mountains, you can find her curled up reading a book or arguing with her husband over the best kind of sushi.

Visit her at www.katiecrossbooks.com for free short stories, extra savings on all her books (and some you can't buy on the retailers), and so much more.